In her latest novel Miss Stern returns to one of her favorite themes: the interlacing of love, hate and lesser emotions in a large and diverse family. She gets inside her family, their humor, their guilt, their fatal tendency to play God with each other's lives.

"Unless I marry I mean to adopt lots of children," said Zillah Collier. And had the opportunity presented itself, she would have—lots of laughing children of all sizes and shapes, all with lives that needed a guiding hand and an anchor to windward.

Three sets of children, united by the marriage of their parents, find that growing up together in a large and happy family is not an uncomplicated business. Zillah, the eldest, is a girl who works at being significantly and recognizably herself every waking moment. She has swung confidently in all her life where others might have felt a certain diffidence, leaving everywhere the imprint of her vivid, Zillahesque personality. Surrounded by, and exuding in large quantities, a disarming love, Zillah wakes to the realization that she is suddenly less than everybody's darling, that she is inexplicably beginning to lose ground.

Slowly these laughing children grow up to face many things—a brother's virtual suicide at Suez, another brother whose relentless judgment results in

(Continued on back flap)

ate mind.

UNLESS I MARRY

G. B. STERN

Unless I Marry

New York
THE MACMILLAN COMPANY
1959

For permission to quote the five lines " People that build their houses inland . . ." from Second April, *copyright 1921-1948, by Edna St. Vincent Millay, the author is grateful to Norma Millay Ellis.*

First Printing

Printed in the United States of America

Library of Congress catalog card number: 59-13361

For
MARGUERITE
STEEN

Chapter One

ZILLAH OFTEN announced, " I mean to adopt lots and lots
of children. Until I marry." And sometimes added in
further elucidation to more sophisticated confidants: " I
must have an adoption complex! " The age of her
indiscriminately adopted children in relation to herself
was immaterial; she had already whaled whole families,
old and young, who on a more positive response than
mere submission, welcomed their enslavement by this
radiant creature with ichor in her veins. . . . Till something
happened (maybe equivalent to that inexplicable Declaration of Independence so prized in the U.S.A.) causing a
desire in them to carry the responsibility of their own
existence with all its disadvantages, and end the season of
benefits gladly accepted. Finding they were no longer
" hers," all Zillah's natural instincts of self-preservation
then rushed in to assure her that she was fickle (an attribute
always quite bearable to the ego) and they could no
longer hold her faithful. She was fifteen-and-a-half when
one of these puzzling secessions must have put a check on
her yen for a family of " adopted " children, to account
for her sheer delight at the prospect of her father's second
marriage; because Mrs. Susanna Morrison, who had
already been twice widowed, could immediately contribute her two younger children, Jackie and Wendy, to
fill the void. What a scoop! For although an only child,

Zillah's possessive instincts were totally free from tiresome jealousy; she had never desired to take the head of the table for any lonely beloved Daddy-figure, reign supreme in his heart, light of his days and apple of his eye: a packet of wistful phrases with no realistic bearing on the truth; and in fact, " You've only got to read Euripides to see what all *that* meant," quoth Zillah sagely . . . and if asked which play of Euripides, flung out: " *Iphigenia*," and left it there, loosely pendant, always intending one day to learn Greek and read up *Iphigenia* for herself—or was it *Œdipus*?

She sat now at the head of his table, ready in a fortnight to yield up this purely honorary position to a cruel step-mother (another silly myth!). Richard Collier had thought it a sound idea to invite Susanna and her two youngsters on a bring-together week-end directly Zillah and Jackie were both home for the Easter holidays from their separate schools. Wendy was still at kindergarten age, though she had been allowed as a treat and for convenience sake to sit up for the occasion, provided she did not contribute too much nursery prattle; her mother had warned her several times beforehand, but Wendy was a silent little girl and it was Jackie who should have been warned, Jackie wildly excited and radio-active; you simply could not ignore Jackie, with far more than his fair share of vitality, his cup never full but at once it had to be spilling over; a few years ago a terse nanny, not the old-fashioned " spoiling " kind, used to remark: " A little less of it, Jackie! People aren't interested in hearing your voice; *a little less of it!* "——Ah, but people were too frequently interested, and discipline perpetually handicapped by the boy's quicksilver charm. . . . And he's beautiful, thought Zillah, exulting; the only one of us who really is. Us, her family now, a permanent endowment.

8

" I can't imagine where he gets it from," Susanna remarked placidly of Jackie's mercurial quality. " Not from me, nor his father as far as I can remember." And indeed, she only had to remember as far back as her second husband's death in 1946, four years ago. Both Susanna's marriages had been pleasant and serene, though now she accounted for the speedy success of Richard's wooing with an entirely apocryphal description: " You see, he swept me off my feet! " Anyone less like a tempestuous lover to sweep a woman off her feet could hardly be imagined, yet an affinity could be perceived between Richard and Susanna, in that both preferred the company of their contemporaries and had more spontaneous tenderness towards a partner in marriage than for any child of their own flesh and blood. Richard was definite and taciturn, Susanna amiable and easily contented, the bloom still on her mind and health in her body; and they had managed to achieve perfect accord over what so often evoked argument and sacrifice even between couples passionately in love: the question of where they were to dwell, in his house or in hers; and then choosing as their future home *a charming modern residence, architect-designed, standing in its own grounds on an upland site with uninterrupted views over the rolling countryside of Mershire* recently bought by Susanna on Richard's advice when she sought him out in his professional capacity as senior partner in a firm of house-agents in Oldbridge; she had intended to buy something smaller and less impressive, but almost at first sight of one another both had realised that her original intention had better be expanded. Richard's Elizabethan cottages, two knocked into one, lay a little way off the road about twenty miles farther east than Cobblers Meadow; and he remarked now, while sawing away at the chicken, that they had had to do some

9

shifting round for the week-end, as Whistle Cottage was a bit small to accommodate such a family: Zillah would sleep on a camp-bed in the sitting-room, vacating her own room, the largest, for Susanna and Wendy to share.

Here Susanna broke in with a contrite: " Oh, dear, if I'd realised you hadn't a spare room I shouldn't have arrived overflowing with children."

Richard grinned at her ten-in-a-tenement word, and Zillah burst out that she simply loved *overflowing*, loved sleeping on a camp-bed in the sitting-room. " It's terribly depressing never to have one's home really full up; and besides, we *have* a spare room in what used to be the next-door cottage."

Which her father supplemented with the nonchalant piece of information that it was usually called the box room and supposed to be haunted. " I don't suppose Jackie's going to mind that, but if he'd rather, Zillah can change with him."

" Mind! " Mind sleeping in a haunted room? Jackie was exultant at the chance; not for anything would he have given up such an opportunity—and he began to boast, little-boy fashion, of how he would deal with any nocturnal apparition, provoke it into such excesses of ghost-behaviour that he would be implored to tour all over the country describing what he had heard and seen. " Oh, Jiminy, I'm glad I came! I wouldn't have missed this—and I'm glad Mummy's going to marry someone with an unlaid ghost in the panelling of their house. Oh, please, please, till I've laid it, *don't* sell Whistle Cottage! " Out of breath he had to stop, still jubilant, his eyes sparkling and the air about him a-crackle with the electricity his wiry, swaggering little body seemed to generate.

Wendy took advantage of the lull to let her voice be heard for the first time during the meal. " Why is it Whistle Cottage? It doesn't whistle. Jackie whistles but cottages don't! "

" The ghost whistles! " cried Jackie, again monopolising the conversation. " I'll hear it to-night down the chimney; nobody's heard it for a hundred years, but *I* will, whistling and howling and skirling. It's a ghost with bagpipes! "

The latter part of his braggadocio came into competition with Zillah informing them all that the cottage had once, long ago, been an inn called The Pig and Whistle. " And some of our ghastly quaint friends, when we moved in, wanted us to go back to calling it that again; but I said and Daddy said that there was no sense in calling it an inn when it wasn't an inn; it would have been pretending."

Susanna remarked that it was a funny name all the same; and she had once lived near a public house called The Goat and Compasses, just as funny.

Richard courteously put her right on the funniness of both inn signs. " The Goat and Compasses is a corruption of ' God Emcompasseth Us,' and Pig and Whistle was originally ' Pyx and Housel '—you nearly always find a hostelry for pilgrims where there's an old church not far away."

" You never told me that, Daddy," Zillah broke in, fascinated at this fresh item of ancient history. " But there isn't an old church not far away."

" There was before the Reformation. It was razed to the ground."

" *Razed!* " repeated Jackie, ferociously relishing his mental picture of razing.

" Gracious, eight o'clock! " And Susanna led her youngest off to bed, promising her a night-light. " As it's your first time ever in a strange bedroom, I bought a box coming along."

" Is she a nervous child? " Richard asked. " She doesn't look it." He meant that Wendy looked stolid.

" Oh, no, not as a rule, but she's really only a baby still, so I thought just in case . . . No, Zillah, darling, don't you move; I know my way, and I'll be down presently. And then it will be Jackie's turn," playfully threatening him; " but luckily we don't have to *put* him to bed."

" Don't have to put me, either," Wendy objected sleepily, as the door closed behind them.

" Pyx and Housel," murmured Zillah, to impress on her memory those two words miles out of her usual vocabulary of school and home; " the Pyx and Housel. . . . I mustn't, I simply *mustn't* forget."

" Whenever Wendy forgets anything she wants to remember, she cries," Jackie put in, but giving the item of information not unkindly. " She isn't a cry-baby when she gets left alone in the dark, but she is when she forgets something. Isn't it curious," taking Richard and Zillah into his confidence, " how nobody can help anyone remember anything? But she can't just chuck away what she's forgotten; you see her *struggling* to bring it from her back mind to her front mind, as if it were alive."

" You mean," suggested his middle-aged host, choosing to treat Jackie's final ambiguous statement with respect, " that she can't include forgetfulness into her range of experience, as we do."

" Yes, and let it go at that." Jackie was not pretending; he really had seen in a flash what was conveyed by Wendy's inability to " take forgetfulness into her range of experience," a moment ago on the very tip of memory, and then mysteriously fled into unsuspected folds and recesses of her " back mind " as opposed to her " front mind," and nobody grown-up and infallible could help her, and she couldn't help herself, so she cried.

Zillah and Susanna were in the kitchen after dinner, stacking the dishes and making coffee, and also exchanging confidences in a way that would have been impossible if Ivy, the Colliers' daily, had not already gone home after several good-natured offers to stay and wash up.

" Exchanging confidences " was perhaps a euphemism, for Zillah raced on and on with all the flexible variations that a monologue could offer her, not in bulldozer style, but adoring narrative for its own sake; narrative vivid and inconsequent as though speech were too important to be held up by connecting links. And Susanna, a good listener but not wontedly silent, was too grateful for Zillah's refusal to regard her as a cruel interloping step-mother, to put up any resistance.

" Your small daughter's very particular: she wouldn't let me read her the sort of story-book *I* always loved best —about a large family of naughty children who rush about disobeying the grown-ups and having tremendous adventures and acting plays. . . . I know what you're going to say : that I ought to have gone on the stage myself, and it's true, I *am* the type—that's where I'm right out of character, because I've never wanted to. I did act once at school, in *Candida*: do you remember that scene at the end where she had to choose between Morell and March-banks, and said, ' I give myself to the weaker of the two? ' Shaw's wonderful when he's subtle, isn't he? But Wendy prefers being shown pictures and plumping down her fore-finger on one so that you can't turn the page, and then just waiting, instead of saying, ' Please, what's that about? ' So I hoiked out a lovely book called the *Childhood of Jesus* when He was a little boy, not all hushed and Bible-

language, and managed twice to get her past the Slaughter
of the Innocents, but she always turned me back again, till
at last I unclamped her, and we went on to a picture
of little Jesus having a birthday party and a cake with
four candles and lots of presents, but He had presents
hanging on a Christmas tree as well as piled beside his
plate; Wendy knew about birthdays and she knew about
Christmas, but hers have always been separate and she
simply couldn't understand how Jesus's birthday was our
Christmas."

" You're marvellous with her, Zillah my dear."
Susanna had no deposit of irony in her nature, or she
might have thanked this newcomer of sixteen for so much
useful information poured forth about her own offspring.
" Usually with strangers she wraps herself up in silence
and they can't get through; and she's worse when they
say, ' Will you give me a kiss, dear? ' "

Zillah laughed and said she didn't have to ask for that
reluctant kiss, but had received a long, throttling, wordless
embrace at the end of the Scripture story.

" Yes, Wendy's not clever but Scripture fascinates her;
I'm no good at it so I try and push her on to *The House
at Pooh Corner* instead—Bridget sent it for her birthday.
Wendy was Bride's favourite and Geth loved Jackie
best, one each, so it was quite fair, but Geth was home
only three months ago when he left Oxford to join
a digging party in Crete, and my, how he spoiled his
brother! "

" Oh, Jackie's irresistible! He reminds me of a boy—
well, he wasn't a boy exactly, I met him at his coming-of-
age. We danced and danced and then he proposed to me,
but of course that was ridiculous, I was barely fourteen,
I forget how I came to be there at all. His father drove
me home long after midnight, but it wasn't either of them

who said I was like a tropical bird with flame-tipped wings streaking over the top of the water—I believe why I shan't miss living at Whistle Cottage is because there's no water near enough; I'd adore to have a stormy sea crashing against the wall under my window like the poetess who wrote ' People who build their houses inland——' Oh, bother! I've forgotten how it goes on, and I thought I knew it by heart. Now if I were Wendy I'd cry, wouldn't I, because it's got itself lost behind the front part of my brain——"

Suddenly Zillah's discourse was interrupted by a bell ringing on a shrill insistent note.

" Visitors? " asked Susanna.

" No, that bell rings from upstairs somewhere."

Richard strolled in and filled the hiatus. " Jackie."

" Jackie! " Zillah raced up the stairs two at a time, Richard following, Susanna last on a tranquil " he must have over-eaten," confirming her fiancé's opinion of her as eighteen-carat gold: a mother who did not fuss on hearing one of her children loudly pealing the bell in a strange house.

. . . A little boy, small and thin, with tousled hair and an enchanting grin, and for all his thirteen years looking not a day more than nine or ten, was sitting bolt upright in bed. " I say," addressing Zillah directly she switched on the light by the door, " I *am* sorry; I couldn't make out what the rumpus was about when I heard all of you tearing upstairs; I just thought I was turning on the light when I pulled this; if I'd known it was a bell——"

" This " was a cord dangling against the wall just above his bed, and it was quite legitimate to imagine it existed for the convenience of turning the light on and off without getting out of bed. So he was forgiven, told he ought to be asleep already; and his two older visitors went downstairs again, Susanna far more concerned in case Richard's coffee might be boiling over: Richard must be handed his coffee hot and strong and just right, and a boy of thirteen should be perfectly well able to look after himself in any crisis, were it the jungle or the North Pole or the spare bedroom of Whistle Cottage. It was *men* who needed her care.

But Jackie's youthful hostess remained behind with him. She closed the door and came and sat on the end of his bed. " Hallo, Jackie! " she said, as though they had only just that moment met for the first time. " Hallo! "

Until lately, dread had not been a word needed in Susanna's vocabulary: she never dreaded anything: " Why should I? Things don't matter until they happen." But she had really dreaded the advent of a stepdaughter in her teens who might resent her and be antagonistic and possibly very rude. Neither of her former husbands had already been married with rude, antagonistic daughters to form one of the family and disturb its peace. At sixteen this Zillah would be—what was the word?—adolescent, and Susanna had heard enough of adolescence to wish to keep clear of it. Of course Bride had once been adolescent, and Wendy would be if she lived long enough; but perhaps by then (Susanna reflected hazily) clever men would have found a cure for it.

Nevertheless she had not been looking forward to this week-end which was to be her introduction to Zillah. And now she lay comfortably in Zillah's bedroom at Whistle Cottage promising herself never again to lapse into a state of mind so far from sensible. Because look how beautifully it had all turned out; and how her proverbial luck had held over three husbands (her wedding to Richard was to take place in a fortnight, so already she might safely say "I love all three of my husbands alike"); held like a strong cable, instead of the usual tenuous gold thread most people have to be content with; for instead of a step-daughter situation, she was now awarded the positive asset of this rare and convenient Zillah thrown in as a bonus to relieve her of all future perplexities: a Zillah who apparently understood children and was willing to take them over as her own responsibility. Not that Susanna's children had ever been neglected or met with harsh treatment; she had tried always to be sweet and kind; but Zillah rejoiced openly in their company and they in hers; she managed them and took them over, not merely trying by diffident, useful little services to ingratiate herself; her immediate conquest of Jackie and Wendy had a triumphant quality, though perhaps that was an odd way to describe a schoolgirl, confident and fearless, skimming the stream like a tropical bird with flame-tipped wings. . . . Now where on earth could that apt description have come from? The girl would hardly have mentioned it about herself; and as for Zillah's father, equally one could not imagine Richard ever coming out with any lyrical passage about flame-tipped wings; the only nice thing he had said of Zillah was " She's no fool; on the contrary, she's mature for her age, but she needs drastic blue-pencilling." A little odd that he should be so un-enthusiastic about an only daughter and so undemonstra-tive with her. True, he was generally undemonstrative, but one knew he could be otherwise. . . . Susanna shimmered a little as she lay there in the dark. Perhaps Zillah reminded him too painfully of the mother who had died giving birth to her, and so maybe that was why poor Richard kept their relationship prosaic; and perhaps again (her meditations were frequently interspersed by an amiable " perhaps " or " maybe ") that was why she had

17

grown up no fool, because her brain had been left to fend for itself. Susanna was still a little dazed by Zillah in spate and by the diversity of matter that came swirling down-stream and was past and round the bend almost before one could see what it was; impossible to hope to fish anything out and examine it; but every now and then one could retrieve something worth-while, something really wise and genuine . . . as when she had been scornful of those " quaint " friends who had wanted her father to revert to calling their cottage The Pig and Whistle as though it were still a public house. Natural good taste— a little astonishing; oftener at that age they had natural *bad* taste unless they were colourless and uninteresting, and nobody could say that about her new stepdaughter. " She's not actually pretty, but there's something *very* attractive in her looks! " And then on a sudden dis-quieting thought: " I hope she won't marry too young! " Not that one would wish to deprive a girl of her normal fulfilment as a good man's wife—(or several good men's wife in rotation)—but supposing not only Jackie and Wendy now, but one day Bride and Geth might come back again into home waters, and supposing Bride for instance (Geth wasn't married yet) were to have children and brought them along to be grandmothered, and then—Oh, dear! Susanna had as little desire for grandmotherhood as for motherhood! So please heaven, without exploiting this incredible version of a Cinderella who positively begged to rake out the ashes in the kitchen fire, please find some way to keep her in the family for as long as possible; I wouldn't *dream* of exploiting her, Susanna earnestly assured the oblong strip of latticed moonlight which was the window of Zillah's bedroom in Whistle Cottage; it's right for a woman to marry; Susanna was an addict for weddings; both her other marriages had ended happily; her first husband dying in his sleep, one of those how-wonderful-for-him sort of deaths after very little previous suffering, and her second spouse killed instantaneously in a train accident. Compared with a long-drawn-out break-up by desertion or divorce, what forbearance Fate had shown towards her. " And I'm too old now to give Richard children," she reflected furthermore, temperamentally neither mother nor mistress but a wife. And with nothing to dread in the familiar experience of wedding-night and honeymoon, all was well in the most benign of all possible worlds.

". . . Hallo, Jackie! " On this greeting, gay acknowledgment of a special alliance between them, Zillah sat down at the end of his bed, after the others had gone, and invited him to come clean. She didn't say " a little less of it, Jackie," not she; " a little more of it, Jackie," was nearer the mark.

Of course her intuition had heard at once in his apology the hint of laughing it off; and known the moment she saw him sitting bolt upright in bed, his thin charming body in its white pyjama jacket outlined against the dark, worm-eaten panelling, why had been his sudden urgency of desire to pull the bell-cord and summon familiar faces and even a tangible scolding in a familiar voice, rather than—fear of the ghost. Ingenious young Jackie! That was quite a plausible fib he had thought up, of having believed it was the light-cord dangling behind his bed, but Zillah guessed that to a boy with his type of wide swing-over from boasting to frantic fear, there might be ghosts everywhere. Swaggering at table was all very fine— " Oh, Jiminy! I wouldn't have missed this! "—but lying alone scared out of his wits by his own over-vivid imagination was not quite so funny; so of course he had to devise a ruse to bring human company rushing to his bedside.

She acquitted him nevertheless of boasting to show off; the earlier mood had arisen from his buoyant conviction that thus things were; until now, the pendulum had beat over to the opposite extreme, and now he still kept on pretending that was it *likely* he'd have rung any old bell for any old family to come trooping upstairs with all that silly fuss and chatter—Holy Moses, no! " The *last* thing I wanted! I wish people had some sense: why, it might scare the ghost away! "

" It might, Jackie, it might; and then you couldn't write it up for the papers afterwards, could you? Would you like me to tell you the legends I've heard round about here, with all the lurid details? "

At which he had knocked over the glass of water they gave him on his declaration of being so terribly thirsty. . . . " Oh, bother! "

" Here, I'll fill it up again," she teased him.

" No. I've drunk enough."

" But, Jackie, you hardly sipped it, I was watching you."

And still he stood out—while she waited for him to stop putting on an act. Then suddenly caved in: " Please, oh, *please* may I have a night-light, like Wendy? "

. . . When Zillah left him, however, he was again as brave as a young lion, scornful of such baby palliatives. She lay wide-awake on the sitting-room divan, and congratulated herself on her daring methods with Jackie and their magnificent results; with nothing but impatience for those grown-ups who, had they suspected his lapse, would have soothed his terrors with an indulgent: " It's *quite* all right, darling. Look, I'll draw the curtain and let you see there's nothing behind. Of course there are no ghosts. We'll leave the door open and here's your night-light. Give us a nice kiss—*there's* my big boy! "

Susanna had said of Geth that he had adopted Jackie, but Zillah, intoxicated with her handling when presented with a complex psychological problem, could not think highly of this night-light spoiling from an old-fashioned, lumbering, though no doubt well-meaning Gethyn Dymond. You must *never* aid a child to escape from reality by the soft glimmer from a floating little round candle-boat in a saucer. As for her father's platitude: " He's a boy, so he won't mind the haunted room "— what a hope! So she, Zillah, had chosen instead to march Jackie straight up to face a panic until now nebulous and unformed, thereby cocking a snook at this old-fashioned lumbering though no doubt well-meaning elder brother. Apparently Jackie used to coax a sort of strong-man reassurance out of Geth's presence, who would certainly at this juncture have given in with a half-laughing " Oh, well, I suppose you must have it then."

But the man dormant in a boy of thirteen would be insulted later on if he had to remember her concession to his babyish fears. Lucky for him that someone more up-to-date and psychologically wise had triumphantly taken over from Geth. Boasting was of course a symptom, and as such she had encouraged it, not checking even his most outrageous declarations: " It isn't always conceited to boast "—and then told him stories about famous boasters: D'Artagnon, for instance, Gascon leader of the Three Musketeers, and Alan Breck, and Fluellen, and St. Paul. And who besides herself, reflected Zillah, would be original enough to physic a youngster of thirteen by sitting on his bed and quoting St. Paul?

And then he had exclaimed, as though on a discovery: " You're the leading lady and I'm the leading man! All the rest are everyday people, but not us, not you and me, we're special! Zillah, Zillah, ZILLAH! " he chanted. " Zillah's coming to live with us for ever and always except when we're both at school and that won't last long now. I don't want a night-light when I can have you, and you're much nearer my age than any of the others; I'm thirteen-and-a-quarter and Wendy's only a baby. Mummy told me I was to be more with my temporaries, and I asked her what temporaries were and she said ' friends of your own age, dear! ' But you won't want temporaries, will you, if you've got me? "

Zillah thought delightedly how in one evening she had become indispensable to Susanna and Wendy and Jackie. And then perhaps one day those other new relations of hers, Geth and Bridget, might have children and bring them within her range and she would adopt them too . . . until she married and had lots and lots of her own. She was in that mood of eucharist to the present moment which of course must go on and on for ever, so that she could not stop reliving her conquests, quoting to herself frag-ments of what they had said, evidence of how they had wanted her. " Temporaries " . . . she laughed at Jackie's sums in simple subtraction; why, Susanna who was thirty years older than herself had already become her firm friend; and Wendy, nine years younger; at first she had made a set at Wendy, because she was such a plain little thing and might therefore be the weaker of the two, needing her more (like Candida's husband), but presently she realised it was beautiful, charming, independent young Jackie who was the real dependent . . . Jackie, suddenly whistling what he called the Zillah-tune, a wooing little song-without-words that seduced her heart. Sensible? Of course not. Who cares about being sensible? . . . " You're the leading lady and I'm the leading man."

. . . Yes, in spite of his little-boy status, in spite of his earlier coaxing for a night-light——

Zillah suddenly spoke aloud in the dark. " We're going to be lovers one day! "

There was no moon shining in when he woke hours later, all his courage trickled away, choking with fear, the room thick with darkness—a *haunted* room—he was quite sure he had not woken of his own accord. He couldn't look at his watch because he'd have to get up and go across to the door to switch on the light before he could see in this terrible room they'd given him; the light couldn't be turned on by the bell cord dangling just above his head, he knew that now—Well, he had known it before, but you can't do it all twice, tug it and pretend to be surprised when human voices and familiar footsteps came running up to see what you wanted; not twice, especially as Zillah had guessed the act he'd put on for valour's sake.

A sudden spurt of resentment: she might have given him a night-light; she used all her power *not* to allow him to have one; Uncle Richard said Zillah had it all her own way, and no wonder, you couldn't prevent it! But it wasn't fair—" Whistle Cottage is just as strange for me as for Wendy, and then they had to go and put me in the only horrible haunted room, and I'm the youngest of all of them except Wendy, and she's sleeping with Mummy so she's all right. Zillah *might* have let me have a night-light; Geth would have in a moment "—his coaxing had always worked with Geth; and in the dormitory at school eight of them slept together. But when you're nakedly alone the bogies get in. . . . Worse than bogies, much much worse, and it's as if you'd never felt brave before and never will again.

" It's no good trying to escape," Zillah had said; " you must face it out and fight it out, over and over again," and then told him . . . There it was again, that noise, creaking and creeping nearer; not exactly the noise, but the not-noise she told him about, creeping nearer! If he'd had a night-light it wouldn't have dared come through the wall while he lay there, stiff and clenched in the thick dark, remembering every detail. . . .

Jackie could bear it no longer; he sprang out of bed and stood for a moment breathing hard, then padded on bare feet to the door where the switch was, turned on the light and left it burning. At a slower pace, already reassured, he went back to bed, thinking " she won't see it, even if she's awake too and goes to the window; she's sleeping in the sitting-room, and that faces the other way." And then when morning came and directly he awoke, he could easily turn it off. One always felt quite different in the morning. Always? But he'd never been put to sleep in a haunted room before. He glanced at his watch —only ten past two—it seemed as though he'd been awake for hours and hours.

Now that panic had subsided at the consoling sight of the furniture and his clothes thrown down on a chair, he began to recover something of his excitement over Zillah. Nevertheless, he wished she hadn't guessed his secret; it cramped his style and made him feel a fool and years and years her junior, instead of only three years. He'd have to prove his intrepid quality all the more, but in a different place, so as to re-impress her. What he'd have liked (getting comfortably sleepy now that all was well) would have been for them to have let him stay up a bit later and allotted him a camp-bed in the sitting-room; and with his mother and Wendy occupying her bedroom, for Zillah to have imagined she would like to try the haunted room, just to see if she met the ghost; and *then* come rushing down to him hours later, waking him up; she'd be madly frightened and he'd encircle her with his protection: "All right, you sleep here, and I'll lie on the floor"—only of course it wouldn't be the floor—he'd be beside her on the narrow camp-bed, suddenly a man, leading man to her leading lady.

Chapter Two

SUSANNA'S NEPHEWS, Don and Barry King, took delight in teasing her over her ritual preparations for the impending marriage of her younger son Jackie and her beloved stepdaughter Zillah; they called it " Auntie's Fourth Wedding," and it was true that Susanna had really missed the congenial flurry of this special sort of festive occasion. Though she was placidly devoted to Richard Collier, her third husband, theirs had been a very quiet wedding six years ago, and it seemed a long time since she heard the voice that had breathed so cheerfully over her two previous Edens.

But Heather, her seventeen-year-old niece who had left school rather young to " run a home for my brothers " (they had less complimentary names for her advent!) rebuked their good-natured teasing; said she thought Aunt Susanna was being terribly nice over not kicking up a fuss over Jackie at nineteen being far too young to marry, " besides not *nearly* good enough for Zillah." For Heather's unblinking devotion to Zillah, who had enslaved her when she first came back, surpassed even the tremendous partisanship of the rest of her little group of disciples.

" One could hardly expect his own mother to kick up a fuss over Jackie not being nearly good enough! And anyway, why the heck can't Aunt Susanna let them have a quiet wedding with just us there, and a few pretty garden flowers on the table, and some nice lemonade, instead of planning to stir up the whole countryside for miles round with the bell-ringers practising day and night and Cobblers Meadow a shambles."

After a moment's pondering, Heather said: " She wants to make Zillah feel she's welcome in the family."

Shouts from her brothers: as though *Zillah* required that! Zillah, reigning princess of the house of Collier. " Most mothers *would* say that nineteen was too young to marry, and tell them they'd damn well got to wait for a couple of years till Jackie came of age."

" If there's a war with Nasser, and he gets sent out and killed, he won't ever come of age. It's all very well for you two, you've done your National Service, but Jackie's only half-way through his. Besides, he looks a lot older than nineteen, and that makes all the difference."

" Don't see why. In the dark all cats are alike."

Heather stared at him, round-eyed. " Barry, what *do* you mean? " (She was always saying Barry what *do* you mean?)

" My little moss-rose, we wouldn't rob you of your dew, not one single drop of it; time enough when *you* get married and we have Auntie's Fifth Wedding. Anyhow, it's all to the good that our Zillah isn't making a splendid match with some South-American tycoon who'll cover her with diamonds and take her away from us for ever; at least as Jackie's wife she'll be at home and in the family where we never stop wanting her."

After a long pause when the slow chugging sound of her mental machinery could almost be heard working, Heather produced To-day's Great Thought: " I believe *that's* why Aunt Susanna hasn't felt that he's too young to marry; because we never stop wanting her here. But no ty-typhoon could ever be as beautiful as Jackie!"

And even Barry had to allow that beautiful was hardly an exaggeration in this instance; merely a statement too flat and prosaic to describe Jackie's sort of resplendent quality, his lashes and the corners of his lips and the very bone structure of his ardent young face seeming to curl back; and eyes brilliant as though he had dwelt from birth in some fabulous country that never knew sin nor fear nor the sorrowful experience of coming to terms with life when it wouldn't come to terms with you. He had shot up with his usual impetuosity like a tropical sapling, straight and tall, overleaping the hobbledehoy stage; so visually there had seemed nothing ridiculous in nineteen mating with nearly twenty-three when he and Zillah had burst in on his last leave and in rapturous chorus announced their engagement. " Isn't it all heavenly and *swingeing*! "—bringing to the inadequacy of heaven their own slang of the moment.

" And as for diamonds," Heather went on, " look at the ring he gave her! "

" Yes, he went a big bust on that; good thing he can afford it. If Wendy hadn't spilled the coffee all over Great-Aunt Hannah's pearl-grey satin gown years ago and then had to make matters worse by saying she couldn't help being clumsy because she was so *poss-thumous*. . . ."

For it had all fallen out as Susanna would have planned it; Great-Aunt Hannah dying six months ago, and, in Biblical phrase, without issue, she had originally willed half her money to the R.S.P.C.A. and the rest to be divided between those two little animals of her own kin, Jackie and Wendy . . . until poor unfortunate Wendy had insisted on carrying her that cup of coffee: the stain would not come out from glacé silk, and it had been completely ruined. Jackie, therefore, who was gay and graceful and resembled herself when she was his age (Great-Aunt Hannah said) scooped Wendy's share as well; not a huge sum, but it yielded about £350 a year which would be helpful until he had done his National Service and chosen a profession. So this undivided legacy enabled him to get married. " Because, after all," Susanna went on musing, " Zillah can live at home for as long as ever she likes." But if there were going to be one of those unsettling wars —and it looked very much like it—she might have fallen in love with a colonel in his late thirties, and if America came in he might even be an American colonel, a Southerner whose home was in Louisiana, and then where would they all be? Or Jackie might be annexed out there by some Pharaoh's daughter, dark and glorious. . . . It wasn't like Susanna's imagination to progress with such kangaroo leaps; the Egyptian princess dark and glorious had been Mrs. C.'s idea. October 14th was the date chosen for the wedding, only six weeks off now; she sighed with relief, and went on trying to decide what colour would suit both Heather and Wendy as chief bridesmaids, as well as the four small girls who would follow Zillah up the aisle. . . . Jackie was the kind of boy who ought to marry young provided he didn't choose anyone stately; she smiled at the notion of their Zillah being stately.

And after the tranquil period of her marriage with Richard when nothing had seemed to happen, everything happened at once and Cobblers Meadow hummed with sounds like a bee's epithalamium. The extent of Susanna's abundant preparations did not have to depend on adaptations of space; the architect who had planned it had been addicted to the modern Swedish idiom, large and light and roomy, with huge glass windows opening on to terraces on the ground floor and balconies on the first floor. Zillah, during the Easter holidays of her father's engagement, had been taken over to see the house and declared at once with a long sigh of satisfaction that it was the dwelling of her dreams. " I know I ought to prefer dark old beams and inglenooks and slippery twisty stairs, and steps up and down where one least expects them, and that it's out of character for me to adore all this modern light and air in a house, but I *do*. Isn't it strange to think that perhaps when they built houses in England in Tudor times, lots of people exclaimed: ' Marry, I do fear me this house is more modern than I wot of from the specifications! ' "

Unkind people, hearing Richard Collier was going to live with his new wife and not she with him, suggested that that was what he had been waiting for: a bathroom to every bedroom, and a very comfortable library built out for his hermit occupation when he should retire and devote himself to a hobby as yet unchosen. He did retire four years later, handing over the goodwill of his house-agency to his junior partner, Barry King. " And his daughter living on poor Susanna as well! She can't earn much more than her pocket-money as an unqualified junior teacher at Wendy Morrison's school." But Richard Collier had not the temperament to brood over accusations if they were beside the point; and " out of character " (though unlike his daughter he would not have continually announced it with such relish) he studied the stock markets for light relief and speculated, not rashly but with intelligence and acumen based on what markets had done before or not done before; and the stock markets had responded by bringing him out about level on every year's gambling. Mrs. Cottesmore, who

30

had served the office faithfully and well for seventeen years of her fifty-five, essayed a graceful gesture of resigning when her chief retired, and of finding another job; and presently they gave in to the extent of allotting her a room right at the top of the Brown House where she needn't get in anybody's way, and could take over the housekeeping till Heather came back from school, doing only part-time work for Peeble, Oakes and Collier. But Heather had recently declared in some distress to her Aunt Susanna that honestly she could manage now without Mrs. C.'s well-meaning domestic help, so *please* could somebody—Uncle Richard or Aunt Susanna—drop her a broad hint that needn't hurt her feelings. It had been left to Zillah, however, to negotiate that tricky and too well-watered pasturage of Mrs. C.'s feelings (Zillah could do *everything* better than anyone else, declared her faithful disciple); tactfully pointing out to her that Mr. Don was due for his National Service and a new clerk would know nothing about the personal side of his clients' financial or temperamental history and their requirements, and as Daddy wouldn't want to be bothered any more, who was so well up in it all as Mrs. C.? So if Mrs. C. consented to return full time, let her take Don's place during his absence. " She's a pathetic old lamb," declared Zillah; and Heather, remorseful, did her very best to find Mrs. C. a pathetic old lamb, but was inordinately grateful, nevertheless, to have had her removed from her immediate sphere; Barry didn't mind her, and passed on the more gossipy clients to her desk in the alcove while he undertook all the out-of-door expeditions himself, accompanying clients to the site of where they proposed to build or to view tumble-down properties while he dilated eloquently on their potentialities. Then Don came back, and Mrs. Cottesmore, still full-time, drove *him* slowly mad . . . and it was too late, Barry pointed out, to start telling her that her middle name was Stop-gap. " And she's jolly useful," he added. " Even with you here, we'd have to have another clerk if we hadn't got her to cope."

" A *silent* clerk? " asked Don wistfully.

" Nobody's silent except Uncle Richard. You'd better grin and bear it, Don."

" Perhaps if I asked Zillah? She can manage most things; it's a knack."

" I agree, she can. But knack or no knack, she can't always be shifting Mrs. C. from one job to another. Why does she get on your nerves? She doesn't on mine."

" She couldn't, you haven't got any; Heather and I have."

" Well then, why? "

They thought, but it was difficult to define for what reasons this cheerful, assiduous, obliging little woman with anxious teeth should have this effect on them.

" If only she wouldn't pounce on any picture paper that features some glamorous brunette running off with somebody else's husband, and insist on reading it aloud to us with comments about having once been herself ' a great one for the boys.' . . . Last time, I said politely that she must have been a regular nymphomaniac, and *nymph* led her miles up the waterways and into the woodlands."

Heather contributed: " And whenever one offers her something that costs about sixpence, ' Oh, I'll accept it, I'm not proud, you mustn't imagine I'll draw myself up to my full height and refuse.' "

" Good lord," Barry exclaimed, " you *have* both got it in for her! If she bridled and said, ' reely I couldn't accept it,' you wouldn't like that either."

And Heather sighed, contrite because Zillah had so

often reminded her that it wasn't much fun to be Mrs. C.

Then in this eventful period at Cobblers Meadow where preparations for the wedding were already jostling and overlapping without orderly sequence, and Zillah, darling Zillah, not selfishly engrossed in her own happiness like almost every other bride-to-be, was able to cope with them all simultaneously, Susanna's somewhat premature " last-minute " activities were interrupted by the return of her elder daughter, minus her husband, after nearly a decade in the eastern hemisphere. Bridget's young step-sister had hitherto been a stranger to her, except from the unconvincing enthusiasm of verbal snapshots in every letter from home; so now, without apparent jealousy, she succumbed to adoption like the rest of the family; though their rapid intimate talks together perforce had to be broken into fragments like an unfinished jigsaw, the pieces picked up anywhere and flung down again as constant interruptions demanded. Squatting one on the bed and the other on the floor, wherever a space could be cleared among the foam and whirl of trousseau all over Zillah's room, Bridget announced on a restless note that she *must* get something to do at once and put behind her the bitter memories of her marriage.

" After the first year I was ' his wife in name only ' as they say," speaking flippantly of her unhappy life with Bertie Rufus Ogilvie. " I fought to make a go of it, but then it got a bit much and I felt I was going right round the bend."

" That was the moment to cut your losses! " Zillah realised that grand tragedy was no more Bridget's style than would have been gentle acceptance of her hard fate.

" I did when I caught myself morbidly on the look-out for digs about my marriage: that old music-hall song—

' I like a fool believed it all; I was an M-U-G! '—I sort of expected people to sing it *at* me."

" Oh, but nobody could be as cruel! "

" Oh, but couldn't they! " mocking Zillah's belief in mankind. Then subsiding. " Though I don't know why the hell I should have minded an extra like that, but the small things do more damage than the big ones; Mother's going to tackle me about being your Matron of Honour; I heard her say to Richard, ' I think Bride would feel left out of it unless we asked her! ' "

" Bridget, darling, I do wish you hadn't just landed yourself into all this extra fuss and hullaballoo of my wedding. If only I could turn down the volume, or tell them I'd changed my mind and wanted a Registry Office wedding, I would."

" I know you would, my lamb. And think of the questions they'd ask! ' For *Bride's* sake? But Bride's enjoying every moment of it!' Ironic, don't you think, that everybody at home should still be calling me Bride, as though I'd just floated down the aisle on my husband's arm! I was christened Beryl Bridget, so they really go miles out of their way in their determination to be inappropriate."

" It would be even more awful if they kept on correcting themselves. Besides "—Zillah produced balm and ointment for at least this smarting place—"St. Bridget wasn't the orange-blossom kind of bride, she was a virgin saint and became Abbess of Kildare."

Beryl Bridget laughed: " You're not suggesting I should found a Convent and rise to be Lady Abbess, are you? "

" I believe you'd be super, my sweet, but I only meant your inside needn't twang like a banjo any more when they call you Bride."

Beryl Bridget Ogilvie seemed oddly comforted by this

alien slant on her name; though she only said: " There's the phone ringing like mad; bet it's for you again."

—" I'll have to get something to do or I'll go bats!" she repeated later, standing in the long grass under a Blenheim orange tree in the orchard and impatiently shaking a branch.

And from half-way up a ladder, Zillah promised with her usual reliable enthusiasm—a contradiction in terms if applied to anyone else—" I'll get you fixed up!" Of course she could get Bride fixed up. " What's your line? At a guess I'd say you'd got it in you to be a simply wonderful organiser! Here, take the basket, I'm coming down. . . . A *wonderful* organiser," she repeated.

" I've never organised anything in my life. Before I fell for Bertie and married him, I trained for the stage."

" How funny! Everyone tried to make *me* take up the stage professionally——"

" I had a chance then of getting into a first-class repertory company——"

" Wasn't it out of character that the stage never appealed to me? I always said that until I married I'd adopt lots of children——"

" What an ass I was to fling away a career all for the love of a rotter! Does one still call them rotters? I'd hate to be dated every time I opened my trap."

" Even at school when a West End producer saw my *Candida* he said: ' It's ridiculous how many dyed-in-the-wool pros I've trained for this part, yet none of them had what this schoolgirl has without any training at all!' "

So for a while they talked simultaneously, Zillah of how strange it was that the stage had never appealed to her, and Bride of how on the contrary she'd desperately wanted to be an actress but now she was free everyone was telling her that it was becoming harder and harder to get even a walk-on part.

Until Zillah swung in where angels might have had a certain diffidence in treading at all: " Look, Bride, let's face up to it: it was *meant* that you shouldn't go on the stage years ago or now; a blessing in disguise. You wouldn't have been *right* for acting " She narrowed her eyes the better to focus her companion; and thus steadily scrutinised, Bridget lost her false buoyancy and began to laugh as so often people do when no laughter is indicated. . . . " I can always tell; I've an instinct for these things; and I've heard you every now and then burlesquing a serious story to amuse visitors, and you were so determined to get it across that you *over*acted. . . . No, darling, don't flinch, because it doesn't matter. What does it amount to in the end? " And for the bracing benefit of Bridget, she proceeded to reduce a so-called romantic stage career to a mere series of sporadic startings and endings, long gaps between, and then every time having to begin again in a different sort of part in a different sort of place without any satisfying continuity of achievement.

" What a typically Zillah-esque way of looking at it! "

" Of course it is: I *am* Zillah! " And with disarming faith and real delight in taking charge, she began to build up the older woman, persuading her that the role now thrust upon her was capable of expansion without limits: " Far more fun and more credit and more *you* than stodging away at lines written for just anybody by other people!—Hi, Atalanta," she broke off and signalled to Wendy lumping towards them from the house. " We're here; are you looking for apples or for us? "

" How badly Wendy runs," remarked Bridget in an undertone.

Wendy drew up, panting. "*Break-down of discussions between M-Menzies and Nasser!*" she announced between gasps, as though she were a dispatch messenger. "Expulsion of oil officials! In the Bible they're always running short of oil for their lamps—the Ten Virgins did, didn't they, or at least half of them, but who was Ata—Ata——?"

"Attagirl!" put in her sister.

Wendy took not the slightest notice; her eyes were on Zillah. "Aren't you coming in? You're *always* talking to Bride now!" And galloped back again to the house.

"D'you know," remarked Bridget ruefully, "the infant Wendy used to follow me round like a devoted puppy; and when I first thought of coming home, I said to myself: 'I know one person who's going to be thrilled!' But I seem to have fallen rather flat. And lately she carries on as though she personally owned the Middle East."

"Yes, I'm not happy about Wendy."

"Have you a clue what it's all about?"

"It's because she's always had full marks for Scripture and never for anything else," Zillah supplied on an enigmatic inflexion.

Susanna had noticed it too. "Wendy's been so difficult during these holidays," but she spoke with as little concern as if Wendy had been a schoolgirl unknown to her, lately featuring in a newspaper paragraph; "bursting out at meals with those over-excited recitations of names from the Bible—have you any notion what's suddenly the matter with her, Zillah?"

"I believe I have. . . . But I'll get the real hang of it when I go back to-morrow to Sheridan House."

"Go back?" surprised. "Back to the school? But Zillah dear, you've left. You gave them notice at the end of last term. Naturally you had to, with your wedding in October and so much to be settled."

Whereupon, smiling widely, Zillah handed over to Susanna the thousand wedding preparations. "Jackie won't be getting any more leave anyhow till just before the fourteenth." Her manner unregretfully denoted that any girl could stay at home for endless fittings of her trousseau and so forth, but that it took this original Zillah to be gone away for no more apparently dramatic reason than to keep an eye on a difficult little step-sister at school. Zillah in character, Zillah out of character, what matter as long as you heard Jackie's Zillah-tune softly whistled on the air. . . .

"But you gave notice," Susanna persisted. "They all said good-bye and how sorry they were to lose you, and clubbed to send a pressure cooker; so practical of them, except that you'll be living here until you and Jackie can have a home of your own, and so—*Can* you go back now, Zillah, after they've already replaced you with the kindergarten children?"

Zillah hugged her and asserted confidently that whether she'd given notice and been replaced a million times, there would be nothing but sheer delight from Miss Jenkinson over her return at any moment.

"And would you see anything at all of Wendy in Form Four?"

"Enough to find out pretty soon what's wrong.'

"Then you think it's more than just her age?"

And every inch a professional psychiatrist, Zillah re-asserted, "I don't like it " . . . without any reassuring " Don't worry, darling," because so obviously it had not occurred to Susanna, occupied and contented, that any-thing as futile as worry need intrude into her busy days or dreamless nights, merely on the score of the youngest of her four children bursting out with geographical names from the Bible and putting everybody right on the crisis in the Middle East.

For that was the clue, Zillah was sure, these place-names familiar to Wendy from her Scripture lessons with the Headmistress, and now recurring over the air and in the papers, intoxicating her with an unusual sense of power; because her one outstandingly good subject happened to be Scripture; Scripture, not religion. In her other classes she was a dreamy and inattentive pupil, remaining far too long in a junior form where nearly all her school-mates were younger than herself; but lately for the first time Wendy had woken up to what was going on in the great world, conscious of Gaza, Palestine, Mount Sinai, Egypt, the Red Sea, Syria, the Lebanon. . . . What she hasn't grasped, Zillah reflected, is that recognising the ancient names has no direct focus on what's happening transposed to red-hot contemporary problems; the map had changed in the last two thousand years, and what Wendy was longing to proclaim at the top of her voice had about as much topical value as a sick headache. Naturally the poor kid had overdone her enthusiasm and aroused exasperation everywhere; how could anyone help being impatient with a totally unbalanced schoolgirl of fourteen cutting in with her half-baked information, scornful of her family's apparent ignorance, insisting on the wireless for every News bulletin, interrupting every conversation that might happen to glance aside from something to which the whole world ought to give precedence. Full marks for Scripture. . . . Gaza, Palestine, Mount Sinai, Egypt, the Red Sea, Syria, the Lebanon. . . . " That was where Samson——" " That was where Moses——" " That was where the Israelites——"

So Susanna was justified in heaving a sigh of relief when

her fourteen-year-old returned to school, eager to make herself unpopular there with all the " inside information " she had culled at home.

The first clue Zillah was able to pick up bearing on the theme was when Matron came to her for advice on the secretary's problem with regard to Wendy and the papers; the child apparently felt she must have her own paper morning and evening, and had ordered them from the local newsagents to be sent to her forthwith at the school, arguing defiantly with Miss Scott that if she chose to use her pocket-money in that way and give up sweets and so forth, nobody had a *right* to object.

Winifred Scott, perplexed over how to deal with the irrelevant addition to the Head's papers, of an .extra *Daily Express* with the name Morrison scrawled on the front, consulted Matron: " Twice now, Monday and Tuesday. And Wendy Morrison was quite haughty and rude when I remonstrated with her."

Matron said: " You know Zillah Collier's come back after all, until she gets married next month? "

" Yes, isn't it unselfish of her when the wedding's so soon! "

" Oh, but that's Zillah all over. Shall I ask her what she thinks about Wendy? "

" Do; Zillah's very wise on psychology when girls reach the awkward age."

Zillah was duly consulted and betrayed no surprise. " Look here, Matron, if I were you I'd ask Miss Scott to let it slide for the time being. It isn't actually breaking rules, is it, to order your own newspaper? "

" N-n-no," hesitating; " but don't forget that like all the girls from Form Four upwards, Wendy Morrison has the benefit of a talk on Current Events after Prayers every morning."

" But if she craves for more than five minutes on Current Events, surely she ought to be allowed to have it? "

" And establish a precedent? Suppose *all* the girls started ordering their own papers to be sent up every day? "

Zillah laughed at the image conjured up of the breakfast porridge congealing while the pupils of Sheridan House rustled the pages, absorbed in avid assimilation of the latest dispatches from the Middle East. " But, Matron, even if they did, it's not a shocking thing to be interested in world affairs."

Nevertheless, Wendy was going about looking distraught as well as behaving abominably, and Zillah secretly wondered why she had not come to her with confidences on the first count if not on the second. Yet it would be a mistake to force it; she reread a postscript to Jackie's latest letter:

". . . arrival of an expensive compass in a plush-lined case. That extravagant kid Wendy sent it to me—to help me find my way in the trackless desert, I suppose; last time I saw her she babbled a bit about Egypt and miles of sand without an oasis. Ought I to send it back to her? Compasses get issued from Army Stores anyway if and when required; and she's given us a wedding present already, though I clean forget what it was."

And even the infallible insight which earlier had removed Bridget from a potential career behind the footlights, did not at once assist Zillah to psychiatrise the motive below Wendy's Plimsoll line; except that somehow the gift linked on to her obsession with Gaza, Palestine, Mount Sinai, Egypt, the Red Sea, Syria, the Lebanon. . . .

Shortly afterwards, when Form Four during break was

loud with plans for their stall at the School's Annual
Bazaar in aid of the local Orphanage, Wendy Morrison
looked up from her newspaper and told them witheringly
not to be such *babies:* "Heaven knows what's going to
have happened out there by then."

Thus held up in their normal if limited field of interest,
they stared at her resentfully. " Aren't you helping with
our stall? "

" Haven't time."

" No, of course you jolly well haven't if you go and bury
your head in the papers for hours every day as if you were
a prefect or one of the staff! We're all fed up with your
airs and graces "—the taunting circle closed round their
victim—" if you even half-understood what you read,
there might be some sense in being so cocksure."

" I handed out some of your rubbish at home when my
Uncle Cecil came to dinner; he's an M.P., and he
snubbed me and made me look the most awful fool when
I came out with what you'd said about the Children of
Israel; I had to listen to a lecture on what he called the
contemporary political and geographical situation."

" Yes, and Daddy said you must be the biggest duffer
alive if you supposed the boundaries are still where they
used to be when Moses went up Mount Sinai and Samson
pulled down the pillars at Gaza! "

"Oh, can it, everybody! We all know by now she's a
conceited ass. The point is that I as Treasurer have just
been through my accounts for the stall, and I see that
Wendy Morrison's the only name not ticked off. So
what about it, Miss Morrison? Would you be kind
enough to elevate that scriptural and political nose from
its studies for one moment and give me your attention,
plus, if you'll pardon my bluntness, the five bob overdue! "

Form Four was convulsed. Jennifer really was a scream

when she got going; the way she aped their Form-mistress was every bit as good as that woman on TV!

Wendy turned red and then white; crumpling up her newspaper, she rushed blindly away from her tormentors . . . and all but cannoned into Zillah, who tried to grab her, but she shook her off, swerved into the shrubbery and vanished. Whereupon Zillah went to the Headmistress.

" Miss Jenkinson, can you spare me a moment? "

" Yes, Zillah, of course. What's the trouble? "

" Could Miss Bell take over the Kindergarten again just for their percussion class this afternoon? "

As Miss Bell had been engaged for the sole purpose of looking after the Kindergarten, and had been wandering about at a loose end since Zillah's unexpected reappearance, the Head was willing to agree. Zillah's pregnant voice and manner, however, seemed to invite a question of why she wanted to be set free for that period; obligingly, therefore, Miss Jenkinson asked the question.

" If you don't mind, I'd rather not tell you now: I will some day! "

Zillah found Wendy in a spinney hidden from view near a deserted bank of the river; and, not caring how she fulfilled all the platitudes of childish despair, lying face downwards and stormily sobbing her heart out. At first she could get nothing out of the child except that she didn't care, she didn't care, she was going to drown herself . . . and indeed she did seem to Zillah perilously near a nervous breakdown.

" There's no future in any of this," sternly. " Cut your losses and face up to it."

Thus bracingly adjured—and it did sound very adult and grown-up to cut one's losses, more so than any cosier form of consolation—Wendy's sobs gradually grew less violent, and presently she was able to unburden herself

43

of the whole cause of her misery: how thrilled she had been at first when " her subject " leapt into the foreground, how this had led to the Fourth Form ganging up against her, taunting her with getting it all wrong, chucking her out from her place on the Bazaar Committee because she had been throwing her weight about and making them look fools, as Gaza and the Red Sea were quite different now—" But the names are the same; and—oh, Zillah, then they wanted my subscription and I was the only one who hadn't paid; but I haven't got it, because I've p-pledged my pocket-money for weeks and weeks ahead at Wirrals to pay for Jackie's compass so that you and I could follow him all round the maps in my Bible—all those places I know and that aren't a bit like geography, and now he's written that they get them issued by——" Sobs caused her to become incoherent once more.

"—Issued by the Army Stores."

" Yes, did he tell you? So that was a failure, too; I'm a failure all round and a nuisance and an ass, Jennifer said so, they all said so, they're laughing at me. And oh, I did so terribly, terribly want to be well-informed at last. I'll *have* to drown myself! Please go away, Zillah."

Again Zillah spoke a little sternly. " It's no use ever trying to escape. We've got to fight it out. You're to come straight back with me now up to my room, and I'll get books and maps, and by the time we're through you'll know all about the Suez situation, and where Old Testament names and boundaries are the same as now and where they've gone different. And the other girls will respect you after that; think how astonished they'll be! You'll find it interesting too, while a muddle is never interesting. . . . Come along, Wendy sweetheart."

After a couple of hours' intensive grind on the kingdoms and divisions of the Middle East and comparing them with the map at the back of Wendy's Bible, came Zillah's release with a timid knock at the door. " Please, Miss Collier, can Wendy come for a Committee Meeting if you've done with her? We're rather behindhand on getting out the design for this year's stall."

(I thought she was never coming! I told Jennifer, when I slipped her the five bob, to leave us for one hour after they'd spotted us going into my room, but not for two hours and ten minutes!)

" Yes, certainly, Jennifer. Cut along, Wendy! " And on a joyous reaction from grief, suicide and madness, Wendy sprang up, all eager schoolgirl again, full of plans with Jennifer: " Suppose we make——" " Yes, and s'pose we make——" " Tell you what we *must* make——"

The two ran off happily. Zillah heard their voices resounding down the corridor; and depleted, felt the oddest desire to chatter about her trousseau, say with Celestine-the-House-for-Chic. . . . talk of nothing else but clothes for quite a long time.

" How you could *bear* to stay away with all this going on! " exclaimed Susanna, welcoming Jackie's Leading Lady into the eleventh-hour mêlée of preparations. " We kept on hoping that after all they'd be able to let you and Wendy off a *little* earlier than we'd said."

" ' Having put my hand to the plough,' " Zillah burlesqued. And indeed, having committed herself to remain at Sheridan House till within twenty-four hours of her wedding, she could hardly have done a *volte face* and come running back to Cobblers Meadow simply because the Wendy problem had reached its climax and solution sooner than she expected; so with good grace she abided by her announced resolution not to desert the Kinder-garten . . . and the superfluous Miss Bell had to remain

45

unfulfilled, picking up odd jobs here and there, and mentally referring to Zillah with silent sarcasm as " my predecessor."

And if the sounds rising from Cobblers Meadow for several weeks past were like an epithalamium, the house and grounds now brimmed over like a cornucopia. From the terrace and lawn beyond the drawing-room windows, a steady hammering announced that the men were putting up a marquee; the buffet would be in the marquee, where Zillah, a proud Jackie beside her, would cut the huge wedding-cake with its complicated iced sugar fantasies on which the local catering firm had gone all out to prove Mrs. Collier had indeed made no mistake in choosing them in place of one of the big London firms. No sooner had Susanna rushed Zillah outside to show her how it was all being arranged, than she rushed her indoors again into the wreck of Richard's study where the presents were on display. For most of them Zillah had written pretty letters of thanks from the daily descriptions sent her by Susanna, but last-moment parcels were still arriving and being unpacked in a flurry of straw and paper by Bride and Mrs. C. and Heather.

" No, darling, you *can't* stop and look at those, people shouldn't leave it so late if they want to be thanked; all these presents will have to be packed up again and stored after the reception, until you and Jackie have a home of your own; but you simply have to come upstairs—fancy a bride who hasn't even seen her own trousseau! We couldn't lay it out in any of the spare rooms because of course they'll all be chock full from to-morrow. . . . At first I thought if we had it in your father's study and used the dining-room for the presents—but we had to have our meals *somewhere*! This house really is not big enough for a wedding "; Susanna spoke with infinite satisfaction, both as to the proportions of Cobblers Meadow and the even more magnificent proportions of the wedding. " Oh, dear, what's this? I'm sure I never ordered them—oh, yes, I did; bring them along here, please."

" Them " turned out to be a consignment of gilt posts to be linked by red silk cords and set up in the hall, signposting the way to the drawing-room where Zillah and Jackie would greet their guests, and to continue along the terrace and down the steps to the marquee. The post-and-scarlet-cord brigade joined the cast of supers in Susanna's production of Mummy's Fourth Wedding, causing strife and argument as they collided with the removal firm who were taking out the grand piano and other obstructive pieces of furniture from the drawing-room to make room for the guests, three hundred odd, who had accepted the invitations of Mr. and Mrs. Richard Collier requesting their presence at the wedding of Mr. Collier's daughter Zillah to Mrs. Collier's son Rupert Peregrine John— (" Who's that dainty morsel for the sacrifice? " Jackie had demanded.)

Mr. Richard Collier had been spending most of his days at the Brown House with Don and Barry; though he must certainly be home all the next day till the moment when he would drive with his daughter to the church because —Susanna's harmless jest—supposing he went off for a walk and didn't get back in time? Imagine the suspense! And everything *must* go right in this wedding, and offer no scope for catastrophe! Besides, Cobblers Meadow being Zillah's home as well as Jackie's, they could not of course spend the Night Before under the same roof, custom and convention demanding that they should not meet till the moment throbbing with expectation when he stood with Barry beside him at the chancel steps. So Jackie, when he got back from camp, would be spending his prenuptial night at the Brown House, and Heather sleeping here instead, in his room, to be useful for running messages in that little car of hers, appendix to Susanna's big Riley. ". . . And I can't think for the moment who'll be looking after their bachelor lunch-party at the Brown House—oh, yes, of course, you, Mrs. C.; very early, please, my dear, because the ushers must be at the church at least three-quarters of an hour before the ceremony, with so many people to marshal to their seats; people always flock to a simple country wedding more than to a smart London affair; they say it's going to be ' so pretty'."

And then Zillah had to hear about the endless discussion with the organist and the Vicar over the choice of hymns and the anthem, and whether Billy Walker, pride of Ruston Copthall's choir, would not crack his voice when he had to sing his solo. " He's going to be fourteen next week. Always a risk when they're that age! " and " I'm not quite sure if I'm glad or sorry I ordered those posts and cords," Susanna continued; " they make it seem more formal, but you *are* Richard's only child, and though Jackie isn't my one and only, it's a long time since Bride got married, and will be a long time again before Wendy can, so there you are ; and to have guests straying into all the wrong rooms when they've kissed and congratulated you and Jackie, not liking to ask where the champagne is but pretending it's the presents they most wanted to see—Look, Zillah, I do think scarlet and gilt adds to the gaiety, don't you? And it's a relief to have Wendy sensible again; you've been a blessing to the family and deserve all this great happiness coming to you. Wasn't it practical of me, I told Mr. Cook at the Post Office to send up a pile of telegrams every three hours instead of phoning them as they arrive, or the receiver would never have been on the hook. I'd better just give these the once-over. Oh, this is *not* a telegram, it's a congratulations cable from my Geth. . . . I wrote him a very hurried letter, but it would only just have reached him in Africa because he's up-country near—I can't pronounce it; anyway he's not coming." Mildly disappointed, for she had had a fugitive hope that her eldest might have timed a surprise appearance, and had even planned his entering speech: "Room for a Best Man? Out you go, Barry! I'm Jackie's next-of-kin." Yet even in her thoughts it didn't sound *quite* like Geth. "Your four baby bridesmaids look ducks in their Greenaway dresses with tucks and flounces and long sashes, and very proud of the mittens you found for them; they'll look exactly like the illustrations in that delicious book you gave me; it was a stroke of genius when you called out just as the car moved off that perhaps we could copy them from there, and now you're the only person who won't have seen Julie and Emma till to-morrow when they pick up your train, and by then you'll be too excited to be thinking of anyone but Jackie."

"Darling, I've been madly excited thinking of Jackie all this time; it didn't matter that I was doing all my thinking at Sheridan House; with the first dream that comes with the first sleep, I run, I run, I am gathered to his heart! "

"Oh, naturally," Susanna could not see any quotation marks, and a young bride unhampered by reticence might well have spoken thus. Then, ruminating like an amiable cow, she produced her oft-digested cud. "But if you'd stayed and been mixed up with every moment of the preparations—there's nothing to compare with it except . . . and that's a different sort of thrill, that's marriage, but a wedding may only happen once, and to have made such a noble renunciation—yes, Zillah, don't contradict me, it *was* noble!—of all this going on here while you were teaching the three Rs in a kindergarten."

... An emissary from the Brown House, Heather in her Baby Fiat, arrived with the sensational news Jackie had just brought them on his arrival: *mobilised and ordered out in three days*—" so if you'll let Zillah come with me now, they'd have one evening and two nights of his embarkation leave together "—thus Heather in deference to Susanna's eve-of-the-wedding conventions; suppressing that Jackie had sent her with no request but a command; "And I'll whizz her back here before midnight," Heather finished breathlessly.

"You'll whizz her back here before ten o'clock, my girl; she'll look completely washed up to-morrow if she doesn't get her sleep out."

Yet no bride-to-be could have appeared less washed up than Zillah when she astonished her family by coming down to breakfast the next morning as though it were anybody's day of solemnity. She threw herself with zest into the final preparations, insisting that of course she wanted to help Heather and Mrs. C. arrange the flowers in church, lunched off a sandwich robbed from the buffet, and after several reminders that it was high time she started dressing and that Susanna and Bridget with Mrs. Taylor (alias Celestine the House of Chic) were already assembled in her bedroom wondering how a bride could allow herself such a bare margin to don her wedding garments, she bounded lightly upstairs and performed a cartwheel on the threshold of her bedroom as a vent to her feelings and because she was so gloriously happy. . . .

Chapter Three

GETHYN DYMOND leant over a low fence at Cobblers Meadow, watching with interest a little group assembled round the farrier shoeing the sorrel pony who had once galloped Jackie and later Wendy round the home fields. He watched them with peculiar interest, because after nearly nine years away from England, he had only been back in the home circle for less than a week, and preferred to pick up his own clues rather than trust in their biased accounts of events and of one another. He thought the little group looked rather charming in the dappled sunlight: His sister Beryl and his half-sister Wendy, his young cousin Heather King from the Brown House, and Barry her brother, and an elderly woman with a cheerful air and anxious teeth whom he dimly remembered functioning as assistant at the house-agents in Ruston Copthall where Barry had been then a junior partner. Chiefly interesting to him, however, was his young step-sister, Zillah Collier, only daughter of his mother's third husband. A vivid-looking girl, he thought, vivid even when as now she stood motionless and as it were holding herself in, listening intently to old Joe as though he were producing something of value to her which she could not afford to miss because she might want it badly later on. The wind was blowing in Geth's direction and he heard disjointed fragments of what the blacksmith was saying, wafted to him over the long grass. Joe's rough-haired terrier, like Zillah alert and watchful, presently darted forward and pounced on something which looked like hard gristle which had just been removed from the middle of the hoof after paring away the horn round the edge, and devoured it with every sign of appetite and pleasure. " That's the frog," Joe explained; " always got dogs waiting round for the frog; it's the tasty bit, you see, and they know when it's coming. Daresay it's a sort of medicine for them too; you can trust a dog to medicine itself with the right thing; instinct, that's what it is! "

Geth was amused to find he had already so far become a part of rural England that he was absently chewing a piece of grass as he idly surveyed the scene: *instinct* . . . had Joe been a man of science he might have called it atavism, as vague as instinct and rather more pompous. Now that he was too lame from a fractured femur to participate actively in any more digging parties, he intended to settle down in the neighbourhood and write up his notes; he had already acquired a reputation which he found mildly astonishing, with a couple of monographs on previous archæological expeditions; he would have dubbed them unreadable by the general public, but his publisher had explained the current rush for technical and realistic reading as a thirst for knowledge in the young of this decade: " They don't read for recreation, you see, but to help them get on! " . . . Geth's eyes returned to Zillah gravely asking intelligent questions about the frog in the middle of the horse's hoof as though they might help her also to get on. Then it occurred to him that it was near sundown and he wanted a drink, so without waiting for the others to join him, he turned away and sauntered towards the house. A little distance from the terrace he saw Don reclining in a deck-chair, giving the lie to that tendency people had to couple him and his brother as though they were inseparable—" you never see them apart "—" whereas," Don had added, " except in the office, you never see us together, and not often there; Barry does the human contacts and a lot of light chit-chat about fine aggregates and dovetail fillets and wood wool slabs on four-inch by two-inch joists furred to falls; and Bride takes the overflow, or when she can't spare time from that old curiosity shop of hers, slings them over to Mrs. C."

" Doing well, I gather? " Geth had asked.

" Who? Us or Bride? We're all doing fairly well, thanks; branches now at Oldbridge and Long Swynton as well as Ruston Copthall: so between them Barry and Bride and Mrs. C. rope in most of the Home Counties west of London. Zillah fixed up all that: she's perceptive, our Zillah: she spotted that Bride had a gift for organising and—what's it called when you know exactly what to say to every client separately and don't treat them all alike? A kind of psychological know-how, I suppose."

" Zillah seems to run you all," remarked Geth, amused at Don's youthful cynicism overcome by the richness of his theme.

. . . Zillah shot past Geth as she raced towards the house, hardly holding up her pace as in an excess of *joie de vivre* she turned a cartwheel before disappearing through the french windows.

Animated barks; apparently the shoeing was over and Joe had thrown his old cap for the terrier to chew and toss in a bacchanalian frenzy. Geth looked back and waited; " I can do with a drink," when Barry and Don and Bridget joined him, Wendy and Heather following with Ross the pony.

" You have to wait till sundown before you drink at Hill Stations in India, don't you? " asked Wendy, suffering from an overdose of Kipling which had replaced her scripture phase. And Geth gently put her right, saying he wasn't that sort of admirable military gentleman in a dinner-jacket, and had never been in India.

" Zillah's run on ahead to fix the drinks and bring them out on to the terrace."

" Yes, she passed me, and turned a cartwheel."

" Isn't she a delicious clown! " laughed Bridget.

" Mmm. Nice of her to clown for my sole benefit."

" Oh, she wasn't; probably she didn't even see you." And astride the wall of the terrace, Heather explained: " She often does it to let off steam when she's alone."

" If she's alone, how are you to know she often does it? " Geth inquired casually.

" She says so. She has to limber up when she's at bursting point with being happy, to be able to start being happy all over again! "

" It would be a riot if we all let off steam in that way, wouldn't it? "

Suddenly Bridget was reminded of a moment more than a couple of years ago when " at bursting point with being happy " Zillah had come in to dress for her wedding. . . . What could have happened to prevent it at the eleventh hour must have been an unspoken question in Geth's mind ever since he arrived home, so the barrier might as well be lifted now:

" We were waiting in her room, Mother and Heather and I and Celestine, to help Zillah into her wedding-dress, and I imagine all of us looking a bit stuffed and solemn . . . because Jackie "—she brought out the name with some difficulty—" Jackie was, after all, very young to marry. Then we heard her running upstairs and she

54

came in on a cartwheel and arrived back on her feet, laughing at all our surprised faces. Do you remember, Heather? And after that, it sort of released something and we could be as flippant as we liked until——"

" Until? Come on, Beryl." Geth deliberately made his voice neither pro-Zillah nor pro-Jackie, but as though he were speaking of anybody's broken wedding and not of a little half-brother who had left his young bride waiting in vain at the church door like the unfortunate heroine in the music-hall ditty. " Come on, you might as well tell me."

" Mother wrote to you about it."

" Yes, a short note; or she may have spread herself in a second letter which didn't reach me."

" I doubt it; she was far too upset. Poor Mother, she just crumpled when she heard the ghastly news that Jackie had vanished."

" *Zillah* didn't crumple; she forgot herself and hugged and comforted Auntie."

" Shut up, Heather, you don't know what you're talking about; you hadn't even stayed with us in the stuffy little bellringers' room by the side porch that brides can wait in when there's any delay before the organ begins the Voluntary. . . ."

" I had so! "

" You had *not*! You nearly drove us all mad with your fidgeting, and then you went outside to pester the photographer to let you take a shot on your own."

Bridget ignored the girls' wrangle. " And I didn't write to you either. What was the use? I expect you were somewhere ' in the interior ' and lost to the world, being a seismographer or an ethnologist or an œcologist or whatever it is you're always so cagey about when your humble sister asks you foolish questions." . . . But she found no ally for her attempt to lighten the conversation; and after an uncomfortable silence, handed over the theme to Barry and Don. " They can tell you more."

" Only up to the moment when we went ahead to the church. Jackie was staying with us at the Brown House——"

Heather broke in again. "Because Aunt Susanna said bride and bridegroom oughtn't to be under the same roof the night before the wedding. If they had been," darkly ambiguous, "perhaps it might not have happened."

" Oh, put a sock in it! " Don impatiently adjured his sister. " If it were going to happen it would, roof or no roof! "

Barry took up the recital. " We were a stag party for lunch; all togged up except Jackie who was still in his old flannels and pullover, and I said, ' Look, my boy, will you be dressed in time? ' because of course he had to be in full fig, and he laughed ' Good Lord, of course. Didn't you know I was a quick-change artist? It won't take ten minutes to throw on my white satin and orange-blossom and veil! ' He was in uproarious high spirits, and knocking back plenty; in fact, even Harry Soutar felt he had to put in an oar. ' Doing yourself rather *too* well, aren't you, for a bridegroom? ' And then Jackie began to boast about what a strong head he had——"

" In point of fact, he hadn't. So as we were ushers, we had to go on ahead, and he didn't come . . . and he didn't come . . . and Aunt Susanna sat smiling in the front pew, and Barry took up his stand as Best Man, and people were saying what a pretty wedding it was. Zillah had to follow last with Richard, of course. The church was packed, and we were doing our ushers' act ' Friend of bride?' 'Friend of groom?' all along the aisles, until I gathered that Zillah *had* arrived, and I began to get uneasy——"

"We didn't know yet of anything actually wrong except that Jackie was late, and I thought he'd been a bit tipsy when we left him, which wasn't too good considering he only had a couple of days' leave for a honeymoon. And the organist kept on playing the Voluntary, and inside the church everybody whispering, 'She's late, isn't she?'— Naturally they thought it was Zillah who was late; but when at last I went out to see if the procession could form up yet with the bridesmaids behind Zillah on Richard's arm, and find out what the hell Jackie thought he was doing——"

In vain Don searched for something which would cut short this painful reconstruction; because his brother had probably not noticed how Geth kept on looking towards the french windows as though it mattered more that his drink was held up than hearing about a wedding held up two years ago. . . .

And then Susanna appeared from indoors, apologising for the delay. "We're clean out of tonic, Geth," she sank into a deck-chair, "and Zillah had noticed you like it with your gin, so she's gone streaking off to The Holly Bush; we couldn't send Ivy, she's so slow, and anyway she's cooking supper; you've no idea how one has to nurture servants these days; we can't get girls to stay unless their young man has a side-car or pillion. . . . Why are you all looking so serious?"

"Barry's telling Geth about Zillah and Jackie's wedding day," Heather filled in an awkward pause. "He'd just got to where——"

No help for it. And planning a bit of quiet murder on his sister when he got her home, Barry picked up on the

57

story. " We phoned the Brown House and there was no
answer, so Don and I drove back to see what had happened, keeping a sharp lookout on the way in case we
passed Jackie. He wasn't at the house, and he hadn't left
a note or anything and never came near the church either.
We hoiked the Vicar into the vestry and explained, and
he was very decent and went back and did his stuff as
briefly as possible, dismissing everyone as though Jackie
had either been suddenly taken ill or recalled by a change
of Army orders, I forget which——"

"——While I slipped out and broke it to Zillah and we
all went home," finished Susanna on a flat note of anti-
climax.

" Did she——? "

" Not a tear, bless her warm little heart; all she thought
of was how to comfort me; I was so ashamed and disappointed, and anxious too, in case Jackie had gone out
of his mind. . . . I suppose you heard from Barry and
Don about him being in such wonderful spirits at lunch,
though Heather said he'd been terribly down in the
mouth on his return the night before, until he saw Zillah.
But Jackie always was mercurial, that was Richard's word
for him; quicksilver, you know; and he'd thought he was
going to have a whole week for his honeymoon, and being
so madly in love with Zillah and wanting to marry her
more than anything else in the world—But to vanish like
that, he *must* have lost his reason."

" When did you hear anything official, and what? "
Geth spoke on a carefully nondescript note, more as
though he could not with decency leave the subject there,
than because he really desired to know.

" Richard found out through the C.O. that he'd joined
the regiment when they went out to Suez; and a week
or two later, that he'd been killed in a skirmish. I forget

exactly. I suppose he thought there was no need to upset me with a lot of details—"

" No, of course not. Never mind, I'll ask Richard myself."

Susanna was thankful to be spared from dwelling further on the climax of her grief and from giving a coherent narrative of Jackie's death, the little she knew of it, but could pass on to several weeks later and the tidings that he had left Great-Aunt Hannah's money to Zillah. " Of course it took ages for Probate to be granted, and by then it wasn't nearly as much as we'd all expected. Zillah had behaved so wonderfully through all her dreadful humiliation." Susanna fumbled for her handkerchief and mopped her eyes. " Quietish and not moping, though not making us miserable either, by a lot of talking and laughing at the top of her voice. So it was only natural that reaction should set in when she heard of the legacy; and it was then that perhaps she went a little wild; who wouldn't? " Geth noticed Don and Barry both looking rather poker-faced at this point, and suspected they might have been part of the " wildness"! " But you haven't told us yet what *you* think of our Zillah, Geth, dear? "

And with the mischievous smile that at moments lit up his stoic face and caused him to look about nine instead of thirty, Geth replied: " Primitive Girl; the only daughter of Adam and Eve."

" I don't seem to remember a daughter," mused Bridget.

" Naturally she wouldn't have been mentioned; females were of no importance in the Jewish race; but she was there, all the same, the very first girl in the world."

" Wasn't Eve? " suggested Don.

But Heather put that out of action: " Oh, no, Eve was a married woman from the word go."

And while Geth silently relished " from the word go " in that context, the others amused themselves by elaborating his fantasy.

" How did she get on with her brothers? "

" Better with Cain than Abel; Abel used to lecture her, but Cain made rather a pet of his little sister."

" Zillah *wasn't* his sister," Wendy spoke with authority. " Zillah was only mentioned once in Genesis; she was Lamech's son's wife, so that made her Adam's great-great-grandson's daughter-in-law."

" Well! " exclaimed Barry after a stunned silence. " Waddayaknow! "

What did she know indeed! Full marks for Scripture— and memory pouring back Old Testament information from Miss Jenkinson's classes. She recalled how after the Suez episode at Sheridan House, she had once asked Zillah whether all her former proficiency was wasted now that Nasser and others before him had completely changed the Palestine scene? And Zillah had replied: " No, not wasted. You'll have a chance to produce it sooner or later, and find it has a stunning effect on whoever's listening; they'll say ' wherever did you pick up that?' "
. . . Yet even then, Wendy struggled with an idea in the dim recesses of her mind that there was something called love-of-knowledge-for-its-own-sake, deeper and more satis- fying than the " stunning effect " of producing specialised information with an air of plenty-more-where-that-came- from; being Wendy, the doubt perforce remained nebulous; and here and now was Zillah's prophecy vindicated. Fluently she went on: " Cain said his punish- ment was greater than he could bear, and he was a fugitive and a vagabond on earth and the Lord set a mark

on him and he went to dwell in the Land of Nod and—and he knew his wife and she begat Enoch and I forget who Enoch begat, but it was Lamech, four down from Cain, who married Zillah and she bared Tubal Cain."

But Geth stuck to it, when hilarity died down, that Zillah *was* the only daughter of Adam and Eve and that after a good deal of bearing and begatting (according to Wendy) her descendant " four down from Cain." had been named after her because she had become a legend in the family.

" I can't imagine what you're all talking about," Susanna protested, but not quelling them in their nonsense; she liked to hear this light-hearted babble going on around her.

" I suspect that your very first girl in the world liked fruit but hated gardening," Bridget contributed. " She used to plead with Adam to be let off, and as she was Daddy's favourite she could twist him round her little finger; to please him she'd sometimes pick off a pansy head or two, but that was the most she'd do! "

Barry took over the chronicle: " And, *boy*, the row she had with her mother after finding out about Eve's discreditable past, the serpent and sex business. ' How could you, Mummy! ' she raged. ' Letting us in for all this delving and spinning just because you couldn't say no to an apple! ' "

" Whom did she marry, your Zillah? "

" No one. There *was* no one; she died unmarried—"

—A clink of glasses heralded Zillah, bearing a laden tray with shaker, lemon, bottles of gin and dry Martini, and Geth's tonic water.

Susanna relieved her of the tray. " Darling, how sweet

61

of you to bother, and none of us helping you. We were deep in a discussion about the Book of Genesis."

" Not really," contradicted Heather; " though that came into it; actually, we were talking about your name."

Enchanted to have found a Zillah-tune animating the summer air, not even needing to initiate such a congenial topic but to have walked right into it, Zillah flung herself down on the li-lo, shook her head at the cocktail Barry handed her, truly never caring if she had a drink or not (" Yes, it *is* out of character, I know! "), and at once plunged into this richly rewarding theme: Zillah was only her second name, she said, and she had adopted it for general use. Why? Oh, because (with a quick look round, subconsciously wary lest her father were of the group) because really her name was Gail—" And I couldn't live up to it! "

" But Gail suits you! It's an awfully exciting name! "

" Too strong and stormy for me. Like calling a horse Vindictive and he killed her at the brook beside the pollard willow tree. Asking for trouble! "

They had grown accustomed to Zillah's trick of hurling in unidentified allusions without any boring context; and Wendy remarked that she, too, would like to discard her name, it was silly, " But I haven't got a second name, have I, Mummy? "

" No, darling. I thought you'd have liked Wendy because it came out of Peter Pan."

" I wasn't asked; and I'm not nuts on Peter Pan."

" It didn't, it didn't! " Zillah sat bolt upright in her excitement. " Sorry, Susanna, my sweet, but Peter Pan was only a sort of secondary cause. Wendy began with J. M. Barrie's great friend Henley—my head is bloody but unbowed—having an adorable little daughter called Margaret who died when she was only four; and because

62

she used to come running out into the hall to meet him crying, ' Fwendy! Fwendy! '—meaning Barrie was her friend—Fwendy turned into Wendy, and after she died he put it in his play and so a new name was born." She paused, out of breath.

" And where have you kept that one until now? "

" Perhaps she's only just read about it? " laughed Geth —(he remembered skimming a review, on the boat, of a new biography of W. E. Henley, recently published.)

" Oh, things come up or they don't! " Zillah said carelessly. And ignoring the question of only-just-read-about-it—" Unless I marry I mean to adopt lots of children; and the first has got to be a girl and I'll call her Monica; it's my favourite name; Monica was St. Augustine's mother and I know just how she felt about him—I don't care, I *do*! " as the men ragged her on knowing *just* how St. Monica had reacted in a rather different set of circumstances from Zillah's own. While Susanna reflected a little sadly that this was the first time she had noticed how Zillah's " until I marry " had imperceptibly slipped into " unless I marry." " Monica, Arden, Loveday, Nicholas, Dominic—like you, Don."

" Dominic's not so bad when people shorten it to Don."

" If you were a monk," said his cousin Bridget, " a monk of the Dominican order, you'd have to use Dom, not Don, as a prefix."

" But Bride, honey, it's the monks of the Benedictine order, not the Dominicans, who use Dom as a prefix! " Oh, the goodness of Providence in sending her a chance to produce this collector's piece, not to satisfy a power complex, not for the kick of putting someone right, but to watch the stunning effect on whoever was listening.

Geth managed to wait till a member of the group had come in again on cue with an admiring: " How and where do you dig these things up, Zillah!" and then announced loud and clear that he was hungry, hungry for a man's supper, not cocktail nibbles; adding that several minutes ago Ivy had been at the door to signal the meal was ready, but Zillah was in full spate about *just* what it felt like to be St. Monica.

Zillah sprang up, repentant, though from his inflexion she knew Geth was not really cross. She lingered behind, however, and drew Heather back while the family trooped off into the dining-room. " What did Geth say about my name, before I came in? "

" That you were the only daughter of Adam and Eve and the first Young Girl in the world and your father's favourite, and Cain adored you too, but Abel didn't. And Wendy remembered from Genesis that Cain called his great-great-great-grand-daughter after you."

As a résumé of what had transpired, Zillah found this perfectly satisfactory.

Not even Susanna in her mother-capacity thought of mentioning that there were a couple of spare bedrooms at Cobblers Meadow, when Geth announced towards the end of supper that he was not going abroad again, but retiring from active adventure and intended to settle down in the neighbourhood. Somehow, though Geth was her son and unmarried, she could not envisage him staying permanently in someone else's home. And when he went on to inquire if they knew of a suitable small house not too far away (and not too near, but he left out this proviso) Zillah leapt in with: " Whistle Cottage! "

" Whistle Cottage! Of course! " in chorus. And even Richard Collier nodded and agreed that Whistle Cottage might not be a bad idea if on inspection Geth fancied it as a dwelling.

" Is it empty? "

" It will be by the end of the month. I sold it eight years ago to some people called Hart; they paid me quite a decent premium; and now they want to go and live abroad and sell the cottage and, if feasible, some of their furniture with it. Of course, it may not be the style you care for; it's rather a lonely spot, visible from the road, but a long way back."

" I've got a whole album of snapshots," cried Zillah eagerly; " some coloured ones, too; I'll get them, shall I? Or could we drive over now? " . . . They could hear the rain loudly drumming on the roof; the fine weather, too hot for comfort, had broken into a deluge. " Oh, do let's. Why not? "

Her father gave her a few dour but excellent reasons why to-morrow would do; and added that Bridget in her professional capacity had better meet them there. Then turned to Geth and suggested they should adjourn to his study for their port.

" I'd like to see your coloured snapshots later on," said Geth, indulgently as to a child: and Zillah, not resentful but still unconvinced why to-morrow would do instead of to-night, went dancing alongside the two men. " If only I could drive, we'd go at once. I wish I could. I wanted to be the first to show you Whistle Cottage because it used to be my home. Driving's the only thing I've never been able to learn. Isn't it funny, because everyone says I look as if I could drive in my sleep."

" Yes, you're the cat's whiskers. Off with you, my girl! " And with no compunction, Richard sent her packing.

She flung Geth an appealing look and went out, drooping a little—like a thirsty long-stemmed flower, she thought. Who had said that about her? Or hadn't anyone?

" Bride——"
" Yes, Wendy? "
Wendy had waited until they were alone before unburdening herself. " Bride," with her habitual struggle to bring forth a tentative idea that Heather would have blurted out in a moment, " suppose Geth and Zillah fall in love and get married and go to live in Whistle Cottage where she used to live when Mummy first went to Richard's office to find a house and he found her Cobblers Meadow and we're all living in it now."

Bridget helped her. " Yes, it would tidy up into an attractive pattern, wouldn't it? "

" Did you think of it too, before I said anything? Of course they couldn't have the same sort of grand wedding, because of Jackie but they wouldn't want it like that. Geth's not exciting and handsome "—she meant Geth had matter-of-fact agreeable looks not able to compete in the same skies with Jackie's star quality—" but he's not bad-looking, either. And it's so lucky he hasn't brought back a wife nor left a wife out there."

" Not as far as we know. I shouldn't say Geth was a marrying man."

" *Are* there marrying men and marrying women? Separate kinds? "

Bridget laughed and let it go at that.

" Well, then——Oh, Bride, do you think it *will* happen? "

" Perhaps. If it isn't altogether too fortuitous."

" Fort—fort——? "

And Bridget relented: " Too good to be true." For after all, at sixteen it was not culpable ignorance to be unable to define fortuitous, and Scripture, not English, was Wendy's subject; it was she who had evoked for their benefit that Zillah was the daughter-in-law of Lamech who was the son of Enoch who was the son of Cain. . . .

Wendy ploughed on: " If Geth isn't a marrying man, would he ever dare ask Zillah when she's so far above him? "

" She might take the initiative."

" What's initiative? "

" Oh, bother! " patience began to fade. " Sorry, Wendy, but you've got an awfully small vocabulary! "

Behind the closed door of his study, as if half in apology for his summary treatment of Zillah, Richard mentioned to Geth with a laugh how old Colonel Lee-Curtis from Long Swynton was always criticising his handling of a mettlesome little daughter: " ' Gel's altogether *too* mettlesome, Collier,' he would snort, ' needs curbing; discipline, man, discipline's the thing! All those young fellers——' As if I could go round horse-whipping men because of Zillah. I'd never finish! "

" By the way, was her real name Gail, not Zillah? "

" Gale? Good God, no, of course not! Why should I have called my child after bad weather blowing along the south-east coast? Gale! Damn silly name! "

" Oh, I don't know." Geth sounded tolerant. " Not sillier than most names. I rather like it."

But Richard merely remarked: " Well, there's no extra charge for that! " pulled open a drawer and began leafing through an untidy mass of papers he pulled out, relating to the property of Whistle Cottage; both men having tacitly agreed, with the loyalty of a couple of Trappists to the Rule, that they could shelve for the present and then reduce to its barest minimum, the mystery of Jackie's desertion of Zillah on her wedding day and the news of his death a short while afterwards.

At last Richard pushed back his chair. " Better join the others now, or they'll send along one of the girls to see how long we're going to be." Then with a dash of the dry, exasperated humour which his stepson had at once detected: " I wonder what it would feel like to have a daughter with nothing in her? "

Chapter Four

AND IF she knew that only a few yards away from her open
window, here I'm sitting at mine and wondering what the
hell made her say her name was really Gail when it wasn't,
she'd imagine at once I was meditating on writing a
sonnet about her. Or a whole book. And how she'd love
that!

But what's a man to do if he happens to be handicapped by an addiction to bare truth, staying in a house
where daily, hourly, truth is violated and they all worship
Zillah? Worship—God in heaven, let's have an iconoclast
somewhere in the family.

What made her tell us her name was Gail? Oh, as
though it mattered! Let it go at that. In the Zillah
demesne, integrity can't be expected to find a footing
anywhere.

No, that's not fair, one does get from her that startling
flash of truth and wisdom every now and then—not often
—when she ceases to be predictable and utters something
actually objective, actually reflecting no credit on herself:
" When I say, ' I must live my own life,' I usually mean
' I must have my own way! ' " And " Isn't it strange that
we're put on bread and water as a punishment, and on
Bread and Wine as our highest reward! "

Then isn't she able to discriminate between Zillah-
wisdom and Zillah-nonsense? I'd have said that as a
name Zillah was as picturesque as Gail. Yes, but Heather

told her we'd already been focusing on Zillah before she came out on the terrace with the drinks; it was over, and Gail started up something fresh. Then was it just that suddenly captivated by the notion of *being* Gail, she *was* Gail? Her mental processes are amazingly swift; an idea comes out already as an existent reality, and the transition so rapid that she could scarcely have recognised whereabouts they had fused.

Only then they might have asked—yes, I remember, *did* ask why hadn't she let herself always be called Gail? There had to be a reason; and after a losing scuffle on the threshold of fact, it came out plausible enough: Gail was " too strong and stormy " for her . . . . and so the lie crystallised and was accepted by the body of membership then sitting.

Geth flung away his cigarette half-smoked, lit another, and continued to ponder on Zillah, a form of entertainment necessarily incomplete because God forbid that he should summon her in to answer questions.

Poor old Richard, wishing he had a daughter with nothing in her, instead of her profuse strains of unpremeditated art. . . . Skylark—or cuckoo? Cuckoo every time! Hell, I return home and find my whole family under the spell of an affectionate mad girl, her eyes brilliantly happy because she's been able to establish yet another personal affiliation. When or if she can't, she looks as forlorn as if she's lost sixpence; no, worse, as if she'd suddenly found a little hole in the fabric of the universe, and for a moment life was a total loss.

Genuinely affectionate, to do her justice. Not put on for the sake of gaining prestige.

And every single one of them agreed she " behaved beautifully " when—

70

Well . . . gave a performance of behaving beautifully. Heather, loyal young ass, could see no difference; asked " Isn't it the same thing? " Obviously I couldn't go into fine shades with such a dyed-in-the-wool disciple. *Anonymous* is the key word. Would Zillah have " behaved beautifully " if somehow it had been possible for nobody ever to know who was behaving beautifully? If it hadn't borne her signature right across the page?

Come to that, would any of us?

I hope so. I think so.

—When it happened. As good as gold, they said. Not defiant, not bitter, and not putting on a small-wounded-animal act either. I've been congratulating myself on having escaped the drama of Zillah Deserted at the Altar, when to do her justice there was no drama, no *vesti-la-giubba*, no broken heart hidden under a clown's motley.

" You're such a delicious clown, Zillah! " That cartwheel stunt! Did she once see it done spontaneously by somebody else, and copied it, and it went with such a bang that it whetted her appetite to go on getting the same reaction from her audiences? She turns cartwheels rather neatly . . . don't believe I could . . . don't believe I'm going to try . . . you can't have two of us turning cartwheels all over Cobblers Meadow.

God, what wouldn't I give to be quit of the whole bloody show! Is it worth it . . . or what about clearing out?

Then what's preventing you?

I keep on saying " to do her justice." I *am* doing her justice. Jackie was their flesh and blood, and Jackie died . . . but none of them know what or who was responsible, so they still see it as though he had injured Zillah and she had " behaved beautifully."

Chapter Five

FREQUENTLY Geth had to manœuvre his escapes from Whistle Cottage while Zillah was " moving him in," but oftener he submitted. After all, it could not go on for ever, being moved in; and once he was in, he would set up timetable barriers, for Zillah respected the kind of work on which he would be engaged: a sober record of his recent expedition with a party under Professor Bowles which had resulted in the discovery of a buried cache in a Viking grave identified as eighth-century, more important than their original purpose of excavating the medieval chapel of a later century. Already when he mentioned the titles of his two published monographs, he saw Zillah look potential with good resolutions to leave him undisturbed at certain hours. Presently the first freshness of having a Geth to adopt would have worn off. And meanwhile he felt tenderly towards this mother of his, despite the years of his apparent neglect, and no good upsetting her Zillah-shrine too suddenly. So he watched the girl having a whale of a time deciding what he would require at Whistle Cottage, and what he would have to buy or she buy on his behalf or needn't buy at all because she carried some furniture back again from Cobblers Meadow into her old home; when the Cottage had been sold outright on Richard's marriage to Susanna, most of its contents were put up to auction except these

few selected pieces which after eight years had got rooted
into Cobblers Meadow from habit of the eye, and lately
uprooted for the second time on Zillah's happy assumption
that as it was for her own son, Susanna couldn't possibly
mind! " They've always seemed to belong there more
than here! " Zillah far preferred the family-populated
house to the cottage where she and her father had dwelt
comparatively alone; and thus free from nostalgia for the
past, her pleasure and confidence at being indispensable
to Geth showed forth eager as a child's " I *am* helping you,
aren't I, Mummy? " Of course Susanna was his mother
and Beryl his sister, and the latter moreover in the house-
agent and antique furniture business; he had noticed
Zillah every now and then remembering these prior claims
and courteously delegating the office of supervisor—and
then, as often as not, taking it back again. It was during
this period that he began to discover the quantity of
dramatis personæ attached to Cobblers Meadow and the
Brown House, and spreading outwards from intimate
contacts into widening circles, not only via Zillah but
from the rest of the group who (except Richard Collier)
uncritically enjoyed the society of their fellow-creatures;
and whenever they added one more to " the body of
membership," they never dropped another to even it up.
At moments Geth cursed his fractured femur which had
perforce thrust him out of the company of men who did
not need company.

Therefore, when the Third Programme invited him to
join a discussion by four of their party on those excavations
which had aroused such interest among the public, he
accepted thankfully, though it seemed to him hardly
necessary for nearly all the population of Mershire to
assure him at every opportunity how they would not fail
to listen in, it would be highly interesting if a little too

technical for them, and how proud they were at having such a distinguished man in their midst. Geth was no learned churl of the type that occur more often in fiction than in fact, so again he lazily resigned himself to what could not be avoided, and made a mental note that if the talk were to be recorded, he would make sure of not having to listen in, gathered round the radio at Cobblers Meadow with his mother and sisters and Zillah, his cousins, Mrs. Cottesmore, Ivy, and several of the Colliers' most intimate friends. Then the B.B.C. rang up to say that the Curator of the Tusconian Museum, who had been engaged on classifying the hoard, had to go abroad several days sooner than he intended, so the programme, after a quick run-through, would go straight on to the air. " Aren't you nervous? " " Nervous, no, why should I be? " " *I* should be wild with nerves." " Oh, I'm sure you wouldn't when it came to it." " Nor afraid of forgetting your part? " " Well, you see, I haven't got a part! " Dialogue with variations repeated *ad lib* until his departure for London, with a word of commendation to Susanna for not being " wild with nerves " on his behalf.

" I don't see any reason why either of us should be nervous; only I can't help wishing you'd write instead a really interesting story, and were going to read it aloud on the wireless. You write in the sort of way that goes with the sort of story I'd enjoy; because of course I've never been able to get through those books of yours you never sent me—so I bought them—and I did wonder why you always chose such dry *subjects*; no wonder you called them monographs instead of stories. It's such a waste, not using your talent on something readable! "

" Mother, darling, if I wrote a biological monograph with Richard for my *subject*, and even calling him Richard, do you think you could read it? "

" Of course, if it were my Richard. It's when you call them Minoan kings of ten thousand years ago. Why do you kiss me like that as though you were very fond of me? "

" Because I *am* very fond of you, darling; and for your sake I'll try and sound as though I were telling a story about Richard instead of excavations from a Viking grave."

Returning earlier than he had said they might expect him, he went straight to Whistle Cottage, fairly certain of a couple of hours without interruption from Zillah; for by now she had arrived at the chummy stage of asking: Shall we have this here? Where shall we move this? This doesn't look right standing across that corner, does it?

He had chosen for his study the small panelled room at the far end of the cottage, which the Colliers had mostly used as a box room, or occasionally as an extra bedroom; and insisted more firmly than over the rest of the furnishing and decorating, that it would need nothing in it except bookshelves, a filing cabinet, and a huge desk with a lot of drawers. Zillah nodded sagely " —And one really good picture on the wall above the old fireplace. What are you smiling at? " " Nothing, my dear." He settled for the One Good Picture, literally and artistically, and let it go up on the wall; and it *was* a good picture but too appropriate; anyone coming in would probably remark "how appropriate! " evidence of Zillah's concern that everything must conform to his non-existent standards of masculine " rightness." So now he intended to take it down again, thus avoiding argument, persuasion or the sight of her sorrowful surrender.

But stopped short on the threshold, for there she sat installed at his desk, her back to the door, engrossed in making entries into a small notebook ruled for accounts. "Hallo!" said Geth, making the best of it. "I didn't expect to see you here."

She turned with an exclamation of high delight at his early return: "I thought you wouldn't be back for hours, but I couldn't wait till to-morrow, could I, to tell you what I thought of the broadcast?" Geth stiffened his sinews. "Your voice," she began, and amazingly was silent for a moment, knitting her brows in an effort to concentrate. "Your voice . . . it sounded light and pleasant and amused . . . and somehow a little apart from the other three, as though you didn't expect to be taken seriously even though you *were* serious! Of course this is only the way it came over to an ignorant listener. What did you say?"

"I said you were no fool, young woman." And to reward her for actually achieving an impersonal criticism, he decided to leave the One Good Picture on its hook. Seating himself on the end of the desk, he inquired, "What are you doing with all those lists and counterfoils and Bank statements? I'd have sworn you're no good at figures."

"You'd lose your swear," Zillah laughed, gratified at his interest. "I'm as good at figures as an Accountant in the Bank of England. Oh, I know it must seem out of character, but I am."

"Then you're wasted here; you ought to *be* an Accountant in the Bank of England; they'd enjoy having you there."

"I'd rather stay down here with my own tribe. Most women do get worried over accounts and sums, but I find them refreshing when they're complicated and difficult but work out in the end. They seem to promise me that I exist in my own right."

" You must remember I'm slow on the uptake," said
Geth. " I don't quite see why they should."

" Well . . . sometimes when I'm in bed and not asleep,
I don't count sheep jumping over a stile as Nannie told
us to do, their faces are so irritating after the first hundred
thousand, but I *do* count. I count the number of friends
I have, first those over twenty-nine and then under
twenty-nine; or sometimes men and girls divided; and
sometimes just all my male and female friends lumped
together; it's interesting to see if they add up to exactly
the same, or if I've forgotten three or four, or got any new
friends since I last did it "—Geth noticed that she
omitted—" or lost any friends since I last did it," so
presumably she never did!—" Or I count my scarves:
I don't mean I get up and go to the drawer and do it,
but I've got millions of different scarves, and it's quite a
job to remember them all; not the rather dull plain
scarves people used to wear, there's one I often tie over
my head with little figures prancing about and saying
bon jour in every language——"

" I've seen 'em on you. Talkative scarves! "

" And most often of all since I've had a little income of
my own—you know that Jackie left me his legacy from
Great-Aunt Hannah? " She alluded to Jackie quite
naturally without any significant stress of horror or
reluctance—" And when the news of his Will first came
through, I suddenly went gay and on the strength of it
raised an overdraft at the Bank and simply blued money
right and left, telling myself who cares, there's plenty to
come? Going berserk; nearly everybody thinks that's
Russian, I did for ages, but it isn't! " She paused for
breath and for Geth to ask her for elucidation, which he
politely did, though as it happened he was aware that

77

it derived from the Icelandic. " It means wild Norse warrior," said Zillah triumphantly.

" Good. So you behaved like a wild Norse warrior."

" But there was a hitch in Probate."

" There always is."

" And then I got into a panic and cut down drastically, and when at last I was able to pay up some of what I'd borrowed, by selling out shares, and still had a small income from the original capital, I told myself firmly I must live within my slender means. The hardest part of it was presents; you must *never* accept a present without giving a bigger one, that's in the Creed "—her tone implied a capital C—" and charities, I couldn't withdraw from subscribing where I'd promised and they were building on it, simply because I'd been crazy and over-extravagant and optimistic; so it must be me who had to suffer, not them; but I didn't suffer very much," she confided chubbily; " maybe not as much as I ought to have; I managed."

" How? "

" Oh, I had my mother's jewellery I could sell. She died when I was born and I was her only child. I did that first, and then I took a job teaching kindergarten again; not at Wendy's school, at a day school for little boys; and a holiday post helping to run an Employment Bureau; I like that best of all because it isn't only routine work; you discover where the applicants would fit in best, or where they wouldn't even if they thought they would, and sort of direct them into seeing it for themselves."

" Or saying they did."

" No, they really and truly *did*."

" By the time you'd done with them, Zillah, they were too stunned to say anything else."

"Oh, I don't mind being teased," she laughed; "you're a good-tempered teaser, a '*wohltemperierte Klavier*.' It isn't so urgent now about my money affairs because I saved my salaries and saved my income too, and let them all go plonking back into the overdraft; and so my debts stopped looming and menacing and just became like interesting enemies in a war, and I won the war, and I've been terribly good ever since. Would you like to look at these?"—And Geth found his hands full of her lists and accounts and books of counterfoils.

"No," he replied, "I'm scared of your tremendous efficiency; let's take the evidence as read."

"But I want to consult you how to invest my savings, or should I let them lie on deposit? Peter and Michael both advised me to leave on deposit, but Tommy said re-invest, and John, knowing Tommy—well, we all know Tommy!—took me aside and said, ' Look here, Zillah, nothing risky; blue chip Industrials are always bound to be safe.' "

Peter and Michael and Tommy and John . . . off went Zillah into a delirious saga of lovers changing and over-flowing, lost and replaced, during her period as a wild Norse warrior. Affairs of the heart? He remembered from Victorian storybooks that dashing young girls were teased about their " admirers," and the term had been applied literally—they *were* admired. But their equivalent of the 1950s, had they indeed been Zillah's " lovers " in the modern girl's acceptance of passion bound to fulfil itself? And was she taking for granted that of course they were and he knew it, or of course they weren't and he knew it? Either, of course, would fit.

His reflections ran alongside her confidences, not closely attentive to all these Christian names. He could not visualise their owners beyond a tumble and a scatter of

Tommies and Johns and Michaels, and (he thought) more than one Peter; nearly all males of their generation were called Tommy and John and Michael and Peter—he noticed no Davids were included in the cast!—and it was impossible to keep track or separate one from the other, especially as she alluded to them without any explanatory footnotes, dates or cards of identity. Once or twice he asked which was which, referring to them collectively as " your scalps." He learned that his previous surmise about Barry and Don figuring in Zillah's wild period was correct . . . and another " boy-friend " in the county called Robert, nicknamed Robbikins, Little Robber; Geth's bemused mind seized on to Robbikins with relief, for there was only one of him. And a Brian who, so she said, kept on and on ringing her up with the plaint: " What's this wide world to me? Zillah's not here." According to Zillah, and Geth had no reason to doubt it, each rose to be top favourite, and then when his time was up, fell away without bloodshed. . . . " You'll always be my greatest friend." " Perhaps one day when we can afford it——" " I adore you, it's been divine, it's been Heaven, but we'd make each other frightfully unhappy." " We weren't in love really, we only thought we were." If any of them passed out of her immediate ken and presently fell for another girl and married her, Zillah's report was wholly without jealousy: " I don't know the first meaning of jealousy," and Geth was inclined to believe her. And every boy-friend she quoted appeared to be equally uninhibited, and all expressed themselves in hyperbole. Did she have that effect on them, and would he, Geth, presently begin to be equally unreserved and talk to her like all the Tommies and Johns and Michaels? An alarming thought, and he put it from him.

. . . You can listen to this sort of thing for a specified

measure of time, but not for ever, and Geth began to have a feeling of *perpetuum mobile* about the pagan rites of Zillah's berserkery, and saw no reason, if nobody interrupted them, why she should ever stop. And suppose nobody ever did? So lacking the blessed certainty of rescue from outside, he came to his own rescue; aware that if you say " talking of " with sufficient conviction you can nearly always hypnotise the other person into believing they had indeed been talking of.

" Talking of ancient feasts of fertility, I heard from Chris the other day——"

And no need either to specify; he knew several Christophers, and Zillah of all people would hardly notice the absence of a surname. Besides, no actual Chris within his ken had recently been—" surf fishing in the Pacific, and he caught a perch, and as he dragged it in, it started to give birth to an enormous number of baby fish *straight from its body*."

As he had foreseen, Zillah was instantly fascinated, lips parted, eyes raised to him so as not to lose a single word.

" But I thought," she objected, " that fish operated from spawn or something? "

" So did I; but ichthyological research has now established that fish in the Pacific, though nowhere else, do sometimes give birth from the body like that."

He saw her mentally docketing this gleaming moidore; when occasion was generous—and occasion always did seem generous to Zillah—it would doubtless be produced on cue; not cut and dried, but informed anew with her warm-blooded adoption, as during England's Empire-building period, on a swift personal preference they took a liking to an island here and there in an archipelago of islands, annexed it and coloured it red, coloured it Zillah. ... He wondered if he would be present on that inevitable

81

occasion to hear her remark casually: " Chris told me that when he was surf-fishing in the Pacific . . ."

" Is this the sort of thing," Zillah asked, " that your book's going to be about, only not with fish? The book you'll be starting so soon here at this desk which you won't let me ' clutter up,' as you call it, with sealing-wax or even an inkstand, though ink's not clutter and if you write with a fountain-pen it has to be refilled, doesn't it?—and a calendar with slide-in slots for the months and the number of days in the month—Geth, don't be a beast, as if I'd saddle a man with a calendar showing wee doggies playing! I mean just a solid plain useful affair. May I give you one as a Moving-in Present? Let me! "

Dryly he reminded her that she had given him three Moving-in Presents already.

" Well, then, as a mascot to the new book? "

" Lay off, Zillah; I don't need to know the number of days in the months while I'm writing a book."

" I wish one day you'd write a book about *me*." (Ah, and here it was! Only three weeks delayed since he had first been expecting it.) " Do! I'd love it! After you've finished this proper book. I promise not to mind a bit whatever you say."

He smiled and shook his head. " I couldn't do you justice, my dear."

Chapter Six

Mrs. C. came along to Cobblers Meadow with a rich vein of gossip concerning a new client, a foreigner, who had that day been sent on by another house-agent with several orders to view suitable properties, including Whistle Cottage. " Silly me, of course I ought to have seen that it wasn't left on any list when Mr. Dymond bought it, but to tell the truth Messrs. Stone and Wentworth had quite gone out of my head. However, I don't really think that Whistle Cottage would have been quite large enough for this Mr. Chellyvah; he talks of having had a ' landslide,' I suppose he means ' windfall,' and though he's been a townsman all his life, he says, in Vienna and then in London, intends to do everything an English country gentleman would do. Mrs. Bride "—she set Bridget's teeth on edge by invariably calling her Mrs. Bride, half-playfully, half-respectfully—" Mrs. Bride wondered if you'd care for me to take him to inspect Jake's Parcel? They'd be your nearest neighbours there, but half a mile makes quite a difference, and I think you'd find them an asset."

" Depends what you mean by asset," said Richard, deciding to have a conventionally English reaction against foreigners with landslides. But Zillah came to the rescue: " I won't have him laughed at; I expect he's adorable." And quoted three foreigners from her repertoire of lovers-

and-admirers, Karl, Bruno and Jean-Marie, who had all been adorable.

" Then will *you* look after him, Miss Zillie? "

Zillah paused for a moment, tempted. Geth was amusedly aware that he was in danger of being sloughed; and remained silent, waiting on Zillah's decision, which when it came was wholly creditable: with a little sigh of regret that two such helpless creatures should overlap, she shook her head and told Mrs. C. that naturally Mr. Dymond must still have her undivided attention until she had finished moving him into Whistle Cottage. And so as the other partners in the firm of Peeble, Oakes and Collier had their hands full, she would hand over this oddly named Mr. Chellyvah to Mrs. Bride.

And did nothing of the sort. Not for the world would Geth have missed the sight of Zillah " handing over " the newcomer to Bridget nor to anyone else; it simply meant that she multiplied herself to meet the demand so that each client had a whole Zillah functioning on his behalf.

A short while later, following the signing of the lease by Adelbert Ladislas Czelovar, but preceding his actual arrival, Mrs. C. announced with all the relish of a messenger creating alarm and despondency, a rumour that he intended to keep geese, five hundred geese.

" Five hundred geese!" protested Cobblers Meadow separately and in chorus. " But he *can't* keep five hundred geese! "

" They'll make the most ghastly row! "

" Do you remember when we had Antony and Cleopatra in the lower meadow as an experiment? We could hardly hear ourselves speak, and that was only two. But five hundred! A goose fanatic! "

" I'm afraid of geese: they rush out gabbling and attack

you. We'll have to give the short cut a miss, when we walk from here to the Brown House."

Heather was not the only one to be afraid of geese rushing out at her and gabbling; even Barry remarked that he might put up a better show with five hundred tigers. And Susanna, rarely given to exaggeration, wondered if they would have to move away altogether; the prospect of five hundred geese (of whom several would undoubtedly be ganders) half a mile away and only just out of sight beyond the ridge was altogether too formidable a threat for even her serenity; she began trying to assess how far the noise would carry through the still air and over the tree tops.

"They may not all gabble together at the same time," said Barry, trying to take a hopeful view; "but if only half the five hundred have inherited the instinct daily to save the Capitol. . . ."

Agitation subsided when a day before the advent of the Czelovars with five hundred geese in train, Zillah discovered a law was in existence forbidding persons to keep more than five geese to the acre.

Adelbert Czelovar, sandwiched between a merry little daughter of ten and her merry old grandmother, proved to be a middle-aged widower, thin, rather gloomy, scrupulously polite, not a comic stage foreigner in anything he said or did; mistaking a landslide for a windfall must have been, Zillah would have said, right out of character, for his English was excellent.

And they brought along with them, as well as their more useful Lares and Penates, three Chinese geese and one gander.

"How these rumours scamper around!" said Mrs. C., laughing heartily at the credulity of an English village, when she contrived to drop in at the same time as

85

Susanna, who accompanied by Zillah and metaphorically with card-case in hand, paid her duty call at Jake's Parcel. Chuckling, Madame Czelovar informed them over the coffee pot which took the place of tea, that her son, so ambitious always, planned to start a housing estate for bees; the word hives eluded her, but doubtless there would be comfortable accommodation for at least five hundred. And his activities were to extend to almost every other form of livestock reputed to lay eggs: hens and ducks and guinea-fowl.

Encouraging his rustic bent for all she was worth, Zillah furthermore suggested that the pond on his land could be turned into a reserve for salmon-trout; an exotic idea springing from his mother's account of what their life used to be on their estate in the Salzkammergut, the river abounding in blue trout—" *blaue Forellen,* so delicious when brought in fresh, fresh"—her wrinkled old eyes sparkled in retrospect as though the trout were at that moment being carried in in a trug.

" *Für das Gewesene giebt der Bauer nichts,*" her son spoke sadly.

" For the has-been the peasant will give you nothing," his mother translated for their benefit. " When you know my Adelbert, you will also know he has a proverb for every misery; but we are not miserable, Erda and I, and to reserve a salmon-viz-trout pond, that would be *fabelhaft.*"

Adelbert shook his head; he had inquired about the fish already resident in the pond at Jake's Parcel and they were not at all fabulous; a truly English fish, with a bird-like name—" *Ach ja,* perch! "

Geth had rejected Susanna's hint to knock off work and, as an older resident in the neighbourhood, accompany them on their duty call—" Regionally speaking I'm not in the neighbourhood by about twenty miles "—and thus by his laconic refusal missed the very event which he had anticipated with so much sardonic relish; for if anything could be termed *fabelhaft*, it was Zillah's sheer luck in having *perch* thus fortuitously introduced: " Christopher once told me that when he was surf-fishing in the Pacific, he caught a perch, and just as he was dragging it in . . ." Out came the whole story.

" *Sonderbar*, how you remember these things! When we first meet with you outside the fire-smith where our little Erda is taking her pony, you tell her at once about the frog in the foot of a horse that the little dogs wait to eat; and now, look, we jump to the Pacific Ocean! "

Intoxicated by an appreciative audience, Zillah leaped again like a shining mackerel to the home waters off the Lizard and the Land's End. " They've got watchers posted all along the cliffs, and when they see a shoal coming in they cry ' *Heva*,' and you go out in boats trailing a silver spinner because mackerel always follow any glittering object, and so you bring them in and eat them fresh, *fresh*," hardly aware that she was quoting Frau Czelovar almost to the accent. " Oh, you'd adore fresh mackerel—and pilchards," she added, but too carried away to bother about pedantically separating the Cornish watching for pilchards and line-fishing for mackerel. " You should have settled in Cornwall "—and then, as she remembered her manners—" though we're ever so glad you didn't. But, oh dear, we're bats, we're crazy, all of us, to be living bang in the middle of England:

> *People that build their houses inland,*
> *People that buy a plot of ground*
> *Shaped like a house, and build a house there,*
> *Far from the sea-board, far from the sound*
> *Of water sucking the hollow ledges——*"

And while Susanna had an odd sensation of something familiar and yet far away tickling her brain . . . she and Zillah at Whistle Cottage washing up, and Zillah chanting " People who build their houses inland " . . . Mrs. C. exclaimed:

" Oh, Miss Zillah, what a beautiful, beautiful piece of poetry! Do please go on."

Zillah never found it surprising from whom she evoked an enthusiastic response. " Then you love the sea too? You feel the same? "

" Indeed I do! There's nothing like it, the sparkle and the salt smell——"

" Straddling over a rock pool to watch shrimps dart like shadows, and tiny crabs, and anemones unfolding and waving in the water——"

" You pick up shells, gleaming pink mother-o'-pearl or those that spiral into a point, and seaweed——"

" Yes, but not the flat brown strips your landlady objected to when you brought them indoors."

" We had our own cottage in Cornwall when I was young, so she wouldn't have, but I meant the feathery dark crimson fronds that spread like lace."

" And at the farthest end of the pier a flight of rusty iron steps crusted with barnacles down to dim mysterious echoing caves, underneath-the-pier caves. We must make a date and go off together to do all these things."

" *Ich auch, ich auch,*" cried Erda who had been listening enraptured. " Me too, yes? I have never stood saddle over a pool to watch baby crabs and shrimps and also I have not brought home seaweed in stripes that I must not. You will take me when you go, yes? "

" Yes, Erda, darling, we'll take you when we go."

" It is a promise? "

" Yes, it's a promise."

Her grandmother who had been listening indulgently, explained: " It is all to her *merkwürdig*, because from Vienna for holidays we could take her to rivers and lakes and torrents in the mountains, so water she knows but not with salt. And here where now we live, as Fräulein Zillah has already said, planted in the country yes, but the middle of England. Please, Fräulein Zillah, you will tell us more of that recitation, yes? Or do I ask too much? "

So Zillah gladly recited the other verses, and then Susanna asked whether Erda recited, and this drew down on her head the whole of *Erlkönig: " Wer reitet so spät durch Nacht und Wind——"* And then it was time to go home.

Those who are by nature unobtrusive are usually rewarded by good treatment when they do obtrude. So when Geth heard a car approaching down the lane at the back of the cottage, and looked out and saw it was Susanna, he quitted his writing and welcomed her as though she were a queen.

" But why isn't Heather driving you? " for since their income failed to correspond to the high cost of living, and Richard's " hobby " had had a baddish year, they kept no regular chauffeur at Cobblers Meadow, but summoned Heather to combine the job with her multitudinous domestic duties connected with running the Brown House. Yet to-day the gardener was at the wheel; Susanna had borrowed him for an unheralded visit, not to provoke from Heather a reminder of Zillah's gay orders: " Mind, you're not allowed to come over before we're ready to be ' viewed ' with everything in its place including Geth, and then we'll go together and surprise him."

His mother did not at once let out why she had chosen to be independent, and Geth did not ask: natural on the face of it that she should want to be shown over his new dwelling place which eight years ago had been her husband's home; and as she remembered practically nothing of how it had been arranged then, she refrained from plaguing him with comparisons. Often since his return Geth had reflected that he would rather have been like Susanna than like anyone else he knew; in which case, as she was his mother, it was rather a pity this fifty per cent chance had not been fulfilled.

" And now we've done our formal tour of inspection, I'll get you some tea." But Susanna preferred a gin and tonic; getting tea took time, and Maitland should be back at his strawberry beds—it had been an unusually heavy month for him.

" I didn't tell you," she began, " Miss Jenkinson came to see me last week."

" Miss Jenkinson? "

" Yes, the Headmistress at Sheridan House. She's retiring, and drove round to say goodbye to the parents of all her pupils; so we had an interesting chat about Wendy's future."

" From what I've seen and heard of my sister Wendy, I should say her ' future ' was still a mystery."

" Well . . . she's difficult; not as difficult as she was once, but *difficult*. Zillah's suggesting she could take up occupational therapy. But Wendy shied right away from it."

" Even though Zillah was directing her? " gently.

" Oh, yes "—Susanna's mind followed a backward trail to things imperfectly understood at the time they happened. " When she was in that queer state about Suez, and Zillah had been teaching at the school and given notice—I was surprised they let her come back after the summer holidays, because they'd already got Miss Bell to take the Kindergarten—and it meant Zillah getting home only a couple of nights before her wedding day and leaving us to cope meanwhile with all the preparations that mean such a lot to most girls. But she declared Miss Jenkinson would be absolutely delighted to have her back even if she'd got in a hundred substitutes, and that Wendy came before any trousseau or marquees or unpacking the presents. Wendy had to be saved from despair and no one else could do it. The other girls were laughing at her over something to do with her Scripture lessons. So it was only last week I heard that Miss Jenkinson had *not* been so absolutely delighted and could perhaps have coped with Wendy's problem herself; and how poor Miss Bell also had a point of view; Miss Jenkinson said she had realised at the time—not this time, of course, but two years ago— that she might have said to Zillah, ' Look here, my dear, you've been marvellous with Wendy but she's out of the wood now and we can't have Miss Bell wandering about doing nothing all term and feeling superfluous . . . so don't you think you'd better go back and get on with your wedding preparations? ' But she had thought it would be salutary for Zillah to stand by her commitments. I wasn't at all clear what she meant by that part of it, but Miss Jenkinson is so wise! "

Geth decided not to interrupt by asking for details about " poor Miss Bell " nor by interpreting Miss Jenkinson's ideas of what would be salutary for Zillah; for it was the psychology of Susanna-then as compared with Susanna-now that tantalised him, as though he were reading a detective story and within a chapter of the solution. . . . After a pause he quoted an ancient Chinese law, not altogether irrelevant to his undertow of thought, that if you save a person from suicide you are responsible ever afterwards for their maintenance.

"So you don't agree about a training in occupational therapy being right for Wendy?"

"I think Wendy had far better be left to make mistake after mistake than be influenced by a more positive spirit." Geth's voice was as Zillah had described it: *light and pleasant and amused . . . and as though you didn't expect to be taken seriously even though you were serious.*

Chapter Seven

" It's *important*, I tell you," Zillah declared, inaugurating a family session on Wendy's career. " Family session " rather incongruously included Madame Czelovar and Adelbert, such new friends that they had hardly yet had their wrappings removed; yet as sometimes happens for no logical reason, were immediately gathered into the intimate circle at Cobblers Meadow.

Refusing to be drawn into a similar state of vehemence, Geth lay back with eyes half-closed, and murmured, " Depends what you mean by important? "

" Important not to make a mistake in what we choose for Wendy of all girls."

" Making mistakes can be quite a career in itself. But I've no chance against a girl who has spent years and years at an Employment Bureau directing applicants into occupational therapy or away from it."

Adelbert Czelovar, who had a male preference for objective themes, and regretted when the conversation appeared to veer away from " it depends what you mean by important," brought it back by a twitch of the rope in that direction: " Often do I get envelopes with ' important ' outside and I open them and they are not."

" Advertisements say: ' *Important* offer, only open to readers of this paper '—and then it's usually a bijou packet of detergent."

" Business men tell their secretaries they aren't available to a caller; ' but he says it's *important*, sir.' "

" It's terribly important always to keep your promise to a child," Zillah contributed.

" *Ja*, our Erda, she vill not let you rest, but always ' you *promised* me,' until I take care nearly alvays to say perhaps."

" S.P.C.E.," laughed Bride. " Society for the Prevention of Cruelty to Erda."

" Zose letters, and never vill I learn vot they mean here in England: V.I.P. you often say, and that signifies——"

" Very Important Person," in chorus.

" Yes, yes, so vos I told, but who is to decide when they deserve this awarding? Your Parliament? Your Queen? "

" The Home Secretary," Geth enlightened the old lady, quickly forestalling her son who might have enjoined her severely not to be foolish. And Zillah slewed round to the desk and began to doodle a blotting sheet full of Very Important Persons busily decorating themselves with V.I.P.s. . . . And still doodling, came in with an almost absent-minded " If they don't cash in on it, anyone becomes important by being desperately unhappy."

" Once or maybe twice; not if it happens once or twice a week." Geth's accent of light cynicism concealed how he had learnt to dread these flashes which upset his perpetual question-mark on her authenticity.

Madame Czelovar's bright, dark eyes twinkled from one to the other. Then she used her prerogative as the oldest person present to break off from the subject and inquire: " Your little sister is to train as—I do not remember the vords? "

" Occupational therapist."

94

" Why did our Zillah think it so *important* to decide now before Vendy has even left her school? "

Triumphantly Zillah quoted from her collection, a proverb in old French: " ' *Quant le cheval est amblé dounke ferme fols l'estable!* ' "

To do her justice, Geth reflected—(his mind appeared unable to peel away this tiresome recurring prefix and be rid of it)—to do her justice, the items she produced were never merely informative, with a view to educate her hearers; she originally adopted them with a swift recognition that here was something new and odd and vividly coloured. Only they must not be anonymously conveyed; it had to be she who passed them on; she who was the channel for an axiom that it was not much use to shut the stable door after the horse had escaped!

Wendy came into the room with a suspicious: " What are you all talking about? " which naturally put an end to any further adult discussion on the importance or unimportance of not making a mistake in choosing her career. Rapidly changing the subject, Czelovar inquired why Geth's new residence was called Whistle Cottage.

" Over to you, Zillah," sure that she would come in on her cue before you had time to say Goat and Compasses.

Rippling with delight, she responded to Geth's challenge: " You nearly always find a hostelry for pilgrims where there's a church not far away; Whistle Cottage used to be an inn, and the Pig and Whistle a corruption of the Pyx and Housel."

" *Um Gotteswillen!* " cried Elisabeta Czelovar, hands upraised in protest at such erudition. " Vot a young *Professorin*! How do you unbury these things? "

And Zillah, carelessly tossing admiration aside: " Oh, if you live in the country, you just know them."

" But you didn't just know it," exclaimed Wendy, " it was Richard who just knew it——"

(. . . That night when Mother took her and Jackie to stay in a strange little house to meet a strange man and a strange girl who later became familiar as Richard and Zillah . . . and struck by the funny name, she had asked: " *Why* is it Whistle Cottage? It doesn't whistle; Jackie whistles but pigs don't.")

"——It was Richard who just knew it," Wendy re-iterated, a champion of accuracy. " I remember him telling us; I was seven and allowed to stay up for late dinner."

And Geth noticed that she came out with her con-tradiction bluntly, as though Zillah were trying to take credit where no credit was due.

Susanna first. Then Wendy. Who would be next?

Had she been alone in metaphorically drawing a broken sword to defend Zillah against the world, Wendy would probably never have made her discovery that to be banded together in ridicule was more stimulating than serving in any long-standing Zillah brigade; though for some time she had been conscious of the home front being *boring*. Hard to tell when and how the change began? They were all just as fond of Zillah, of course, the inside Zillah, only lately it didn't seem sacrilege to joke about her, and jokes were ever so much more fun than worship. Heather indignantly refused to come in on what Wendy was still not mature enough to classify as an insidious betrayal; in some ways Heather was still a child, thought Wendy, intoxicated by finding herself for the first time in a majority whose behaviour had an unholy quality too subtle to define.

Family wars can be concealed in a basket of figs. . . .

A fig tree flourished against a south wall in the town garden of the Brown House, more sheltered than at Cobblers Meadow. Zillah was always rapturous over figs; she could consume fourteen and only give up on the fifteenth. " Figs are *my fruit*," thus covering the world's yield. And now they were fully ripe for plucking, dark purplish green outside, deep crimson under their skins; and Heather phoned her Aunt Susanna for Wendy to be sent over by bus and help her cope with them, and, a privilege eagerly besought in past years, she could carry back a basketful especially for Zillah. It wouldn't have hurt Wendy, Heather reflected, to have volunteered for the job instead of arriving hot and cross (a little boy had been sick in the seat just behind her) hinting that to fetch her wouldn't have hurt Heather, not more than ten minutes' drive each way; her tone implying that cousins who drove cars were so unimaginative over cousins who were ignominiously not yet allowed a licence.

And so in a silence heavily charged with thunder and under a gruelling sun, they denuded the fig tree. And Wendy muttered, " I hate gardening."

" Call this gardening? " Heather retorted, lapsing into schoolgirl repartee. Then, good-naturedly hoping to divert Wendy's mind from her return journey in the over-crowded bus lugging a huge basket, and by natural transition from figs, she began to chatter of the Garden of Eden and when Geth had pretended that Zillah was the only daughter of Adam and Eve, the very first girl in the world—" Were you there? I forget."

Wendy nodded: " And Abel used to lecture her, so she didn't mind a bit when Cain murdered him. Pretty frightful she was."

" Oh, well," still with a pacifying intention, " that Zillah didn't exist; Geth made her up."

" Yes, and we were all laughing when the real Zillah came in and wondered what on earth we were laughing at, and we were laughing at *her*."

And suddenly Heather flared up in defence of Zillah, less for anything Wendy had said than because her attitude implied that disloyalty was being condoned at Cobblers Meadow and also here in her own home by Barry and Don. She did not realise you could not make anyone return to loyalty when they were not even admitting that disloyalty had taken place. " Look here, what's all this in aid of? It wouldn't hurt you to remember a few things Zillah's done for you."

" I haven't said anything against her, have I? "

" No, but . . . you haven't said or done anything *for* her either; not even picked a few figs without grumbling."

" I can't be always picking figs," which was not unreasonable but hardly good enough to appease Zillah's staunch disciple, who rummaged in her memory for some specific instances where that ungrateful little beast could be brought to acknowledge her benefits and be ashamed. " I suppose you've forgotten when Zillah asked us, long ago, that if we each had a wish, what would yours be? And you were so babyish that you said win the Balloon Race at the Ruston Copthall village fête and use the money to buy an organ; and you didn't win the Balloon Race but Zillah did and she spent her prize on buying you a lovely little musical box she saw in Bride's shop— only it wasn't Bride's then—to make your wish come true, though why you wanted an organ——! The musical box was an antique and tinkled out its tiny repertoire of tunes, and we passed it round and kept on playing them and never got tired of it."

" *I* got tired of it," retorted Wendy; " and that was Zillah all over; I never wanted an ornamental musical

box with three tunes; I *meant* an organ: a plain common
barrel-organ; the kind that has a monkey in a red jacket
sitting on top. And I was terribly disappointed, only I
didn't tell Zillah."

" A barrel-organ! Doesn't that show again what a baby
you were for your age! Good Lord! You must have been
about eight or nine. Zillah spoilt you; she could easily
have spent the cash on herself or kept the musical box."

" No, she couldn't. At least, she wouldn't have, because
then she couldn't have told the story of what a funny little
thing I was but how she'd understood how thrilled I'd be
when my wish came true even though I hadn't won the
Balloon Race. I heard her tell Geth all about it only last
week. And he chaffed her, and said: ' Do you ever tell
that story without tinkled-out-its-tiny-repertoire? Bet you
don't! ' "

" Well," Heather asked after a pause, " and so what? "
" Well . . . it's evidence."
" Evidence of *what*? " pugnaciously demanding an
answer and not getting it.

If these had been the Chronicles of Zillah in any
historical sense, then this summer of 1958 would later have
been referred to as the Secession Period. Secede: *to withdraw formally from the membership of some body.* The group
from Cobblers Meadow, the Brown House and Jake's
Parcel listened when Zillah with her characteristic *brio*
struck a passage for the trumpet and horn . . . but their
response gradually altered to signify " wasn't that a
pearl!" and "could anyone but Zillah——!" and "wait
for it! " Or if only one of the initiates had been present,
an unhallowed urgency to seek out another in order to
report any fresh and funny manifestation of Zillah putting
on her act. The legend had spread far beyond home

circles, wider and farther than Geth had foreseen: via Bride and Mrs. C. at the antique shop and the house-agents' office, each set-up excellently adapted for an unpaid press agency. And Heather could not fail to aggravate disloyalty by her constant excuses for Zillah: " Nobody else would have gone out in all that sluicing downpour the other night with Leslie Winnoway to hear him make his first speech at some poky little club as dreary as himself. When he came to fetch Bride she let him down, and Zillah offered herself instead because he looked so terribly disappointed—oh, I know what you're going to say, but why should she have, except out of pure decency?"

And Geth had indeed speculated on what Zillah's motive may have been.

Chapter Eight

WHAT WAS wrong? Like a flower-bed where the perennials in bloom appear to be thriving, and then mysteriously droop and fail; and the gardener pronounces a sententious " Ah! " and " shouldn't be surprised "—meditates for a moment—" shouldn't be surprised if that wurn't a mole workin' along under the ground! "

The Czelovars had at first been captivated by Zillah in the old familiar way . . . except that where she was used to allegiance remaining taut, almost at once theirs began to sag. Adelbert especially, though he had never fallen headlong in love with her, had admired her, paid her intelligent compliments, and taken for granted her status with her family and old friends; until influenced by an apparently inexplicable swing-over to the left, he, too, started to bring along his contributions to her undoing; and his compliments ceased to contain any nourishment.

Sooner than could have been expected, Jake's Parcel was ready for a house-warming. Geth had firmly refused to allow any such convivial junketings to mark his entrance into Whistle Cottage, but Madame Czelovar offered no such objection, and had in fact welcomed the idea; Erda, too, was a party-minded child; so Adelbert shrugged his shoulders and said: " *Wie es dir gefällt, Mama* "; and

Richard Collier remarked privately to Susanna that he was disappointed in Czelovar who had seemed a sensible man and master in his own house—"but I suppose one has to humour an old mother more than a young wife?" and Susanna kissed him for the compliment and forbore to point out that he never stopped humouring his young wife.

A whale of a house-warming. And after the guests had departed, the Czelovars and their friends from Cobblers Meadow and the Brown House sank exhausted to rest on the veranda, and comfortably compared impressions of what a rewarding party it had been and how lovely Mrs. So-and-so had looked, and how awful Miss So-and-so; while Heather and Erda ladled up what strawberry ice-cream was left in the bucket.

"And you," remarked Madame Czelovar, flirting with Geth Dymond to whom she had taken a fancy, "already you live at your Cottage and vizout any house-hotting? So quick so quick you move in from your dear muzzer's Meadow, and I am sorry, I, for now you are far avay and seldom ve see you."

"I didn't have to move in at all," said Geth, smiling. "I closed my eyes, and when I opened them again, Zillah had me installed."

"*Ach*, Zillah, vhere is she? All ze afternoon I see her in tventy places, yet not like ze gay humming-fly Zillah; her vings are bright but zey do not carry her up, up into ze air!"

And while Geth silently saluted the old lady's perception, Susanna congratulated her on being "quite a poet," surprised at a foreigner's eloquence as opposed to mere verbosity.

Beginning to flag over her ice-cream bucket, and therefore able to pay more attention to what was going on,

Heather looked up and said: " The Lee-Curtis boy drove her back to Long Swynton in his car to see what this wonderful new thatcher has done on their roof; he's taken prizes for thatching; and I heard Zillah say she'd like to try him for your barn here instead of the man Barry always recommends."

" How will she get back? " Susanna inquired.

" He'll drive her back, of course."

" And then drive himself home again? "

" Of *course*," repeated Heather, a touch of defiance in her voice.

Adelbert Czelovar confessed a little plaintively: " She tried to persuade me that I want to learn how myself to thatch the barn, and that an estate-owner in the heart of England would be happy could he do everything himself; but it arrived nowhere, her idea."

" The grain barn might wait ten years for its roof till you became a proficient thatcher; it's a highly skilled craft." Barry was amused at Zillah's eagerness to provide yet another charming hobby to add to the newcomer's bees and geese and reserve for salmon-trout—though the latter idea, too, had "arrived nowhere."

" Erda! " Czelovar called out suddenly; " Erda, not any more ice-cream." She took no notice. " Erda, do you not hear me? *Erda!* "

" I hate my name," his little daughter objected. " It is ugly, that is why I did not hear you."

Privately the Colliers agreed that it was an ugly name, heavy Wagnerian, though not sufficiently an excuse for ignoring a parental command.

"*Liebling!* " said her grandmother, cosily spoiling her, "*I* vished to call you Mitzi, but your father so devoted to ze *Niebelungenlied*, only ze night before you arrive in ze

vorld had zey gone to *Rheingold*, he *und deine selige
Mutter*——"

" I'm going to change it," Erda announced again,
paying no attention to perhaps a redundant " only the
night before you arrive in ze vorld " . . . " Zillah also, she
thinks it ugly and told me her first name is really Brronwyn;
she say it means white breast, and she say that for her
it is too pretty: ' I cannot live up to it! ' "

" ' My real name's Gail,' " murmured Geth re-
miniscently, " ' but it's too strong and stormy for me;
I couldn't live up to it! ' "

—And suddenly, without explanation to the Czelovars,
the whole Zillah set-up collapsed into shouts of laughter.

As though on cue, enter Zillah, eager and glowing,
followed by a bashful escort whom she presented to
Madame Czelovar as Robert Lee-Curtis—" or were you
already introduced at the party? I always call him
Robbikins—Little Robber—Robert's too solid and worthy
for everyday use, I can't live up to it! "

. . . Then stood perplexed and disconcerted, for her
family and friends still could not stop laughing.

And Geth noticed that where Zillah's stories had previously rushed out in a joyous spate, dating from this
moment of derision and on her increasing awareness that
they had not succeeded in finding a good home they
tended to become more and more fantastic and ill-planned,
with the compulsion to impress on an audience her
desperate need to be recognised as one-hundred-per-cent
Zillah for every moment of her waking life. As they say
of the first snowflakes in early winter, " the snow isn't
lying" . . . And he perceived she was in a state of panic
by the way she forfeited relevance if only she could
manage to bring in what might have been spoken in her

praise somewhere and by somebody, hoping against hope that now at the eleventh hour it would do the trick and make all the difference, reverse this new unpopularity— no, worse, this strange suspicion of jeering in the air— and lift her back to where she had been . . . before he arrived at Cobblers Meadow.

Chapter Nine

Mrs. C. was in a quandary.

About a month ago Zillah Collier had come along to her in the antique shop which happened to be empty of customers at the moment, and told her that posters were up in Oldbridge announcing for September 17th a day trip to Brighton by coach. " Did you see it? "

" I saw a poster, but to tell you the truth, I didn't stop to read it."

" ' Those who intend to go are advised to book their places early.'——Shall we, you and I? And not say anything to the others? They aren't crazy about the sea; they're *inland* people."

And Mrs. C., catching her enthusiasm, exclaimed: " Oh, *let's*! And we can do all the foolish childish things we talked about. Something really to look forward to, and all the more because nobody's to know about it. September the 17th, did you say? If it's not a Wednesday we can change my usual day off; I'm sure Mrs. Bride wouldn't mind if I hinted at some important private business I had to transact and say the man couldn't fit me in on any other day; it wouldn't be altogether a lie if ' the man ' was the driver of the coach," and she laughed merrily.

" Then I'll see about the seats at once; front ones if we're allowed to choose."

" You must promise to let me know how much I owe

you for mine. I'm not proud, but this will be *our* treat, not you treating me; it would feel different, somehow."

And Zillah nodded; she understood: *égalité, fraternité* —and what was the other thing the French were so keen on? Suddenly, however, she remembered Erda, and reminded Mrs. C. they would have to take her too: " One should never break one's promise to a child."

" Won't she have gone back to school by then? " Mrs. C. was not sold on children.

" No, not till the end of that week. I'll treat Erda to her seat."

" No, we'll split her between us. But can we trust her not to tell her grandmother till the day before? "

" Yes, I'm sure we can. Children adore secrets."

And Mrs. C. cried in admiration: " How do you know such a lot about children and their funny little inside ways? Without any experience of—I mean without—I mean that of course Mrs. Collier did have two of her own, didn't she, who were children when you first went to live at Cobblers Meadow—I mean one of her own—no, I mean two. . . ."

Zillah rescued her from floundering among Jackie and Wendy, with: " So that's all settled, and we'll have a heavenly day; pray for sunshine or a gale, but not just dull in-between weather."

How lucky I am, thought Mrs. C., to have found this attractive, fascinating, sensitive, poetry-reciting Zillah Collier, who actually chose her as the nicest company for their very, very special treat.

Then where was now the quandary?

Ever since Bridget Ogilvie had returned, and Zillah had persuaded her into a share in the Peeble, Oakes and Collier house agency and also into running an antique business where the premises had fallen vacant, and more-

over handed over Mrs. C. for an *aide-de-camp* in both places
(" though I'm afraid little Heather King will miss me
sadly to help her over the housekeeping; she's very young
and inexperienced still, and with those two brothers . . .")
ever since then and almost from the first moment, Mrs. C.
had fallen on evil days. She did not mentally refer to it
as hell, she referred to it as Mrs. Bride being " a little
difficult to get on with; one must take care not to get on
her nerves; dear, dear, I'm afraid I irritate her or she
wouldn't always be making fun of me." What it actually
amounted to was that in spite of all her Agag endeavours,
she was perpetually providing material for Mrs. Bride's
devil to work on, because she could never exactly analyse
what might bring it into action, except once an exasperated
" *Must* you always call me ' Mrs. Bride '? " But when
her employer scolded or lost her temper it was less hard
to bear than derision and one's foolish idiosyncrasies
described to friends in front of oneself exactly as though
one had no feelings: for instance, her tendency to hypo-
chondria—" though she always *feels* perfectly well,"
explained Mrs. Bride, " I never get complaints about
what she's *got*, only about what she might get if she exposes
herself to any size, shape or form of germ; she visualises
them waiting and then pouncing to attack her." And
Mrs. C., attempting to turn it off with a little laugh, not
easy when one was trembling all over: " You see, I've
never had whooping-cough nor any other of those kiddies'
ailments; I wish I'd got them over before I grew up, then
I wouldn't bother with these precautions."

" You'll be taking precautions against *twins* when you're
eighty," remarked Mrs. Bride.

And once she had overheard, really overheard, she
hadn't snooped, naturally one didn't snoop, she overheard
Bridget carelessly using a word, *sycophant*, as she entered

the room, and then breaking off: " Oh, hello, Mrs. C.,
I thought you were out! " and added, " I was just saying
I was sick of—" Was it scarlet runners for lunch or the
bad weather? But Mrs. C. was sure that what she had
heard was " *a* sycophant " and not " sick *of* " anything.
Though possibly it hadn't been applied to her at all and
she was making herself unhappy for nothing; but the
doubt kept on nagging till it became a positive misery.
A rather bossy cousin, older than herself though they were
at school together, had always said: " You know, Connie,
they'd like you better if you stood up to them; they'd
respect you more." Yes, but when you've been unlucky
at your first attempt to follow this excellent advice and
"stood up to" Mrs. Bride, it was discouraging to find that
you had been neither liked better nor respected more.
Sycophant. . . . At last you had to look it up in the dictionary
—" flatterer, toady, parasitic person, a mean tale-bearer:
Greek *sukophantès*, informer, *sukon* fig, etc.—informing
against plunder of sacred fig-trees". . . And Mrs. C.
heaved a sigh of relief; ridiculous to insinuate that she
would inform against plunder of fig-trees, sacred or otherwise—there was one at the Brown House!—and nobody
could call her a mean tale-bearer either, nor a toady, nor
a parasitic person; when you tried to make yourself as
agreeable as possible, you might be misunderstood, but a
mean tale-bearer was a definite thing, and she never,
never in her whole life had gone tale-bearing from one
person to another; had she been that kind of woman, was
it likely that the popular, glamorous Zillah Collier, everybody's favourite in their little circle, would have invited
her to come away for a day's secret expedition to the
seaside? Invited her instead of Heather King, for instance,
who adored her and had a car? Mrs. C. was a bit puzzled
why not Heather, but then put it down to the fact that she

herself shared with Zillah this whimsical liking for things you could do at the seaside.

Thus self-esteem argued and was reassured . . . till she began to notice something very odd was going on, *very* odd and mysterious, and nice too: for she appeared to be no longer the butt and objective of Mrs. Bride's mockery; when that lady was shafting her taunts in one direction it led to her being quite gentle and lenient to everyone else in her vicinity, and incredibly the jeers had been diverted from herself and fixed on to (you'd hardly believe it) Zillah Collier! Oh, but it was lovely to be free of it all, even before you had quite grasped where it was going instead. But what had Zillah Collier *done*? Was she aware herself that the Colliers and their group were continually laughing at her? Only innocent fun, of course, yet sometimes even innocent fun could be a little cruel.

And next, from wondering if perhaps she should stick up for Zillah (not that I'm very good at sticking up for anybody!) they began to gather her in on the anti-Zillah league, and once or twice she was able to make a contribution to the innocent fun, and was gratified when they laughed and repeated to anyone who had been out of the room at the moment: " Do you know what Mrs. C. has just told us?——"

In on the popular side!

And quite suddenly she remembered the coach trip. The date was less than a week ahead, and then it would be: " Where are Zillah and Mrs. C.? " Oh, yes, a message would be left saying where they'd gone, saying they wouldn't be back till rather late, saying where they had gone *together*. . . .

You can't afford to be identified with the minority, the unpopular side. Maybe if you were very daring and very loyal and above all, independent—not a sycophant, no, no, she wasn't a sycophant, sycophants were mean tale-bearers! . . . You really had been longing for the seaside, and with such an enthusiastic companion to take the lead in doing all they had planned together—

People that build their houses inland
Far from the sea-board, far from the sound
Of water sucking the hollow ledges . . .

But after that concerted burst of laughter when Zillah had entered the room with Mr. Lee-Curtis, doubt was no longer possible; what a pity she had had to repeat herself about living up to names and not being able to live up to them, when she had said it all before about such a different name. . . . You can't save people from themselves if they will be so foolish, and nor could you help having a sense of humour.

Sense of humour or not . . ." *how* can I get out of it? " thought Mrs. C.

And then came her opportunity to get out of her predicament with honour unimpaired, or so she believed. For after a sharp attack of influenza, Susanna Collier did not recover quickly; and having got Geth moved in and then the Czelovars, Zillah once more had to ask the Employment Bureau to arrange a substitute in her place so that she might see Susanna through her convalescence. Therefore Mrs. C. sought her out, and pretending to be terribly disappointed at the collapse of their plan, but taking it for granted that as Mrs. Collier needed nursing to the extent of Zillah staying away from work, then of course it would be useless and unkind to try and persuade her to be away for a whole day, a long, long day.

During their few snatched moments alone, Zillah did not say much, and quietly gave the impression of agreeing that it would be impossible: " What about Erda? Shall I give

you her ticket as well as mine to dispose of? Or perhaps
you'll want to take her all the same and simply get rid
of my ticket? "

Mrs. C. had forgotten about Erda; she had been
putting first things first. She declared, however, that a
twelve-hour day starting at 8 a.m. and accompanied only
by an obstreperous child of ten to look after, did not appeal
to her, but said that the money for Zillah's ticket and half
Erda's would be faithfully returned directly they had been
disposed of.

" It doesn't matter," a trifle weary of all these voluble
assurances.

" Indeed it does, it matters very much; we're none of
us made of money, are we? We want our *quid pro quo*,
even if it's only eleven-and-nine and half eleven-and-nine."
And Mrs. C. came away from Cobblers Meadow feeling
that their interview had been conducted on her side with
a maximum of tact. And, she might have added, a
minimum of truth.

Yet her desire to catch a glimpse of the sea, a glimpse
for her eyes and a whiff for her nostrils, and maybe a
ripple of small waves over her ankles if the weather proved
warm enough, was sincere and could not be renounced
without an effort to save herself from disappointment.
Came an echo on the wind—" It's important never to
break a promise to a child "—so Erda after all might
provide a solution; she went along to Jake's Parcel and
told Erda's grandmother all about the endangered plan,
and might she perhaps like to take over Zillah's seat on
the coach? These coaches were supposed to be very
comfortable, very comfortable indeed. But Madame
Czelovar had not the slightest desire to take anybody's
seat on any coach to go anywhere; a cosy old lady, she
preferred her own armchair in her own home and

abundant meals from her own kitchen, succulently cooked in the Viennese style, by herself more often than not.

" Our little Erda, does she already know about this day by the sea? "

" I'm afraid she does. We told her not to tell—I mean not to ask your permission till nearer the day, but we had to be sure, Miss Collier and I, whether she would be excited enough at the idea to justify our taking a ticket for her so long beforehand; they get quickly booked up, these coach tours."

" *Ach,* what a *Schemozzle*! " cried Erda's grandmother. And her son Adelbert, entering the room at that moment to say he would be late for the meal as they wanted to finish harvesting the ten-acre field before nightfall, inquired what was a schemozzle, and was told the whole story by Mrs. C., ending with the sentiment earnestly expressed to the effect that it was important never to break one's promise to a child.

After a pause, Czelovar remarked: " Do you not think that when we consider what life may produce for any of us, it is also important that children should learn of disappointments and changes of plan that must happen, and so become hardened to meet them? "

Mrs. C. was never loth to enter into abstract discussion with a clever man; therefore for the moment leaving Erda suspended, so to speak, midway between Jake's Parcel and Brighton, she offered a different opinion: " But where we *can* save them from a feeling of insecurity, the effect on their psyche——"

Adelbert waited patiently, but Madame Czelovar preferred to let her grandchild's psyche rip: " Our poor Susanna, I am so very, very sorry she does not recover yet from her influenza. You vill tell her, yes, if you go again —or no, vait, I vill telephone. But I should have supposed that one of the others in the house just for a day could have been nurse, her husband so devoted, and Ivy—*Na*, it is not my business."

" She refuses to allow anyone except Zillah to look after her," explained mendacious Mrs. C.

And then quite unexpectedly Adelbert Czelovar said that he would manage to take a day off from harvesting, and come along to look after his small daughter; adding moreover, on Mrs. C.'s gasp of astonishment: " We need not concern ourselves too much with her; I have friends who live at Brighton, and have children of Erda's age; I will take her there to spend the day; she will be happier than with us, and we will be more free—*nicht wahr, Mama?*"

His mother approved: sometimes he had ideas, this son of hers, though she was sorry for him sacrificing a whole day to be by the side of this not very interesting and not at all beautiful little woman from the house-agents who had found them Jake's Parcel.

Mrs. C. thereupon produced from her handbag Zillah's ticket and Erda's. " I'll leave these with you for safety, and we can meet where the coach stops. I think, don't you, we'd better be there early so as to get front seats; there may be a long queue, and children do love sitting where they can see the horses "—she laughed at her little joke—" that's what my mother used to say when she was a child and they rode in buses: that she loved seeing the horses! And do you know," chattering on to cover her anxiety because Herr Czelovar had brought out his pocket-book and it would be so embarrassing when he began to offer to pay for the seats; she would accept the money for his own ticket, the one he took over from Zillah—" I'm not silly enough to draw myself to my full height and refuse to take it, because it would be only right that Zillah should have her money back "—but the question of Erda's seat would prove more complicated; she and Zillah were going to treat her between them and each pay half, and one did try and avoid talk about money wherever possible. . . . " Do you know, I once made that joke about seeing the horses when I was getting into a motor-bus with my cousin, and she had no sense of humour and explained to me that motor-buses didn't have horses any more."

Herr Czelovar smiled; and, seeing the price of the tickets marked on them, eleven and ninepence, was just about to hand over (with no embarrassment whatever) the sum of twenty-three and sixpence when Mrs. C. confused the issue by insisting that half Erda's ticket was *her* affair, and only the other half which would have been Zillah's could now be delegated to him. Gravely respecting her scruples, but cursing the need for mental arithmetic with such an awkward sum, Adelbert Czelovar added five and tenpence-halfpenny to eleven and ninepence, and borrowed enough from his mother's purse to be able to give this woman—what was her name?—the exact sum of seventeen and sevenpence-halfpenny without having to go through all the complicated dance steps which he foresaw would be the result of handing her a pound and saying he did not want any change; for then she would have declared that she had to give him change, and would find that she had not two and twopence-halfpenny and produce half a crown and he would have to find change for that.

To be escorted on her expedition by such a distinguished gentleman, envied by the whole coach party, or at any rate the female part of it, what could have worked out better? Not that one was a snob nor a sycophant, but the very word escort pre-supposed a gentleman to look after you, and she had a notion that Herr Adelbert Czelovar would look after her as though she were fragile as a piece of Dresden china. Really, it almost looked like a reward for having been so understanding in the first place about poor Zillah Collier not being able to come!

When her son came back into the room from seeing Mrs. C. to the door, Madame Czelovar expressed her astonishment: " I cannot imagine you mucking in on a joy-ride to Brighton! "—in an Austrian version of the idiom.

Then, after a pause, Adelbert produced a reason which at first might have seemed irrelevant: that he was very fond of their friend Susanna, and sorry that she should have so bad an attack of influenza.

And, still substituting her own idiom, his mother agreed that as far as she was concerned, Susanna Collier had got what it takes.

" And for her husband, too, Richard Collier, I have a great regard."

His mother qualified her regard for Richard Collier; she remarked that he hadn't much to say for himself.

" And her son Gethyn Dymond, not often do I converse with him, but if he lived nearer to us I believe I should find he was a man after my own heart."

His mother indicated, strophe and counter-strophe, that no doubt he was right so far as he was concerned; but for herself, conversation with Geth was often a washout because, *nicht wahr*, you couldn't always be remembering which was his deaf ear?

" And the niece and nephews at the Brown House, they also are pleasant; and the little daughter Wendy will grow up, it may be, into a fine character."

" And Zillah? " inquired Madame Czelovar with twinkling eyes.

" Zillah? " and he smiled back at her; " in every big

116

family has to be a joke—you remember our own cousin
Eugenia Czelovar? But Mrs. Bridget Ogilvie, from the
first day I have seen, has not the instincts of a well-bred
woman, and especially towards Mrs. C.; open unkindness
I have not noticed lately, but——" He shrugged his
shoulders, and having left unsaid that helping Mrs. C.
score over Bridget would be worth a million dollars to the
poor little woman's inferiority complex, he went back to
his harvesting.

They were far enough forward in the queue, when the
waiting procession surged eagerly up the steps of the
coach, to take possession of one seat right in front and
two others side by side about half-way down. Mrs. C.
naturally insisted that Erda should have the coveted seat
in front, contesting Herr Czelovar's polite attempt to
persuade her to sit there while he remained farther back
with his little daughter; and almost at once he yielded, so
that shows, reflected Mrs. C., it wasn't that he would
rather sit with Erda than with me, but only that he thought
I ought to have a chance of a seat with the best view.
Mrs. C. was no fool, and had suffered a few painful
experiences of gentlemen trying to wriggle out of sitting
next to her.

Somewhere just below the Plimsoll line of consciousness
during the previous night, she had settled with herself that
if she didn't enjoy to-day, if things went wrong, it might
just be because she deserved it . . . *sycophant* stood out for an
instant against the darkness. But from the very first
moment everything went marvellously well and beyond
her most sanguine expectations, so obviously it was
intended that she should feel perfectly complacent about
the whole arrangement.

On their arrival in Brighton, they took Erda through the

clicking turnstiles and along the full length of the pier, that curious structure apparently ending in mid-ocean with a cluster of pseudo-oriental domes and mosques and minarets, which the English people, he remarked with mild surprise, accepted as no anachronism but entirely in keeping with what one would naturally expect in an English seaside resort.

" Look," cried Erda, " I walk over the middle of the sea," enchanted with the ring of her feet on the peninsula of boards which had gaps wide enough to show her that land was no longer beneath her; and at the far end they let her run ahead up a stairway to a sort of roped-off place, nautical, white-painted, where the "Captain" in charge let her look at ships through a telescope. At last, when she had had her fill of putting pennies into the slots of automatic machines and setting stiff little figures in motion, her father took her in a taxi to spend the rest of the day with his friends who had a house in Hove and several children for her to play with, returned to where he had ensconced Mrs. C. in a deck-chair in a sheltered place near the band, and gathered her up for lunch at a quiet but recherché little restaurant which sedately announced fish for their speciality—" he must have stopped on his way to engage this table in the window, and oh dear, what an extravagant meal he's ordering! "—then recalled that it did not matter because the first time he had come to Peeble, Oakes and Collier to be shown a selection of houses on their books, he referred to having recently had a " landslide," meaning a " windfall "; that was the only time, yes, the only time she had heard him slip up in his scrupulously correct English.

The loveliest mackerel, so fresh that their skins were still sparkling from the sea; true to her obsessions publicly derided by Mrs. Bride——Oh, but Mrs. Bride should see her now!——she never felt safe eating certain sorts of fish when living as far inland as Mershire, but here it was part of the treat, the treat as she and Zillah had planned it all—poor Zillah!—never mind about Zillah!—forget about Zillah!—such bad luck, though, that she couldn't have come too, because after all it had originally been her idea, and she would have loved it so and asked so many eager questions about this delicious white wine in its long slim bottle. Politely Herr Czelovar showed Mrs. C. the name on the label when she asked, and told her how to pronounce it. She thought complacently that he glanced with approval at the clothes she had chosen for the occasion; and indeed, Adelbert had noticed with a certain surprise and relief that most incongruously Mrs. C. had a dress sense and what she wore was exactly right.

After lunch and coffee—" no thank you, no liqueur for me "—they sauntered along the esplanade towards Hove where the beach was comparatively empty; for the high season was over, despite the fine weather dealt them by providence so that they did not have to huddle in shelters from the rain. Then Mrs. C.'s impetuous desire to be on the very edge of the incoming tide led her to run down a short flight of broad wooden steps, Adelbert following. Who would ever have thought one could play all those barefoot games with Mr. Chellyvah that one had so eagerly planned to do with Zillah: idly throwing pebbles to skid along the surface of the sea—" we called it ducks and drakes when I was a girl "—leaning against the breakwater to shy more pebbles at a stick with a battered old pail stuck on top: an Aunt Sally competently improvised by Adelbert. Then she sat down with him on the bottom step, warm with the sun, to put on her stockings again, " how much nicer than deck-chairs! "—she threw a contemptuous glance up to where three ladies of her age sat and knitted beyond the rail of the esplanade. Then idly they watched two children who were solemnly digging with iron spades where the pebbles had relented into a patch of sand; one of them dug a small pool and the other dug a small pool, and then they joined them up, and the result, unmathematically, was a pool much bigger than two pools. "Look at the *Jungling* with the kite," said Adelbert; a boy running along with the wind, the kite-string taut in his hand tugging like mad, silhouetted between them and the seas beyond till he and his kite were tiny dark shapes against the westerly sky. Mrs. C. sighed contentedly, and one thing leading back to another: "They always say in sentimental songs, don't they, how music conjures up memories, but for me—I dare say I've always been funny over little things like when I picked up shells and took them home in my pocket, the way sand had stuck to them and weeks later came dribbling out in a sort of dry cascade."

"You lived beside the sea when you were young?"

"Yes, in a Cornish village on the coast, and even when I had to go away and earn my living I rushed back home whenever I could, and walked along the jetty where it curved round to make a harbour, watching the boats ride and rock on the tide and the men bringing in their haul of lobster and sometimes pilchard or mackerel, and their nets draped over the wall to dry, and the gulls wheeling and screeching and squabbling overhead—I expect you must be thinking me terribly romantic; and then I spotted that pair of cups and saucers for sale in our antique shop in Oldbridge—it wasn't run by Mrs. Bride then, she was still with her husband in Singapore and I worked in Mr. Collier's office——"

Adelbert surveyed the post-impressionist jumble she had

UNLESS I MARRY

presented, and from among the squabbling gulls and the
haul of pilchards in the nets, instinct led him to select the
cups and saucers for further elucidation. Mrs. C. turned
a little coy. " Oh, it's an old story now, and besides it
would take too long, I'd have to explain about the
Balloon Race and—good gracious, it can't be nearly four
o'clock! Our coach starts back at seven-thirty."

" I must break it to you that I'm afraid we will be home
too late for Erda's bedtime if we stay here till then, so I
have hired a car to fetch us and we will be leaving at six
o'clock; it is not good she should be overtired, returning
to school to-morrow. But even then," he smiled, " you will
not need more than one hour and a half to tell me about
the Balloon Race."

" Well, they caught my eye at once in the window of
Mr. Warren's shop, blue and white, with views on them
of well-known English beauty spots, nooks and crannies
and cottages. I knew they would be expensive, but something drew me inside and I asked him if I could look at
them, and you'd never believe it, but at the bottom of the
cup where you'd see it every time you finished drinking
your tea—but I'd never have drunk out of them at all,
they were much too good!—there at the bottom of one of
the cups was a picture of the very harbour where I used
to stroll every evening with——Oh, I won't tell you his
name. Silly, isn't it, to drag in names when you don't
know the person? Besides, José sounds so ridiculously
Spanish for an English fisherman, except that you do find
plenty of Josés in the West Country; you ought to visit
Cornwall some day, Mr. Chellyvah, when you feel
inclined for an unconventional holiday! He was a very
superior fisherman, mind, though even then my father
said I'd be marrying beneath me; anyhow, it all came to
nothing. . . . She was a horrid type of girl, but I wasn't

121

going to *fight* for him, and men get so easily allured by curly black hair and very dark, flashing eyes. Well, you can understand, can't you, though it was years and years afterwards and I'd got over it, how terribly I wanted those cups and saucers to put up on a shelf in my own room and let them remind me—I haven't many ornaments from the past, and I was reading the other day about an old lady ending her days in a most luxurious Home for the Aged, but what she valued most was a cheap alarm clock that she'd brought along with her; it was her *own*, you see. Of course I wasn't fretting over José any more, and I certainly couldn't afford those cups and saucers—Mr. Warren was very kind and said he'd have sold them apart if he could have, but he was hard up too. And then came our annual Village Fête at Ruston Copthall: they always had it on the Saturday before August Bank Holiday—I've still got the ticket for the Balloon Race—I told you I was romantic!—it cost half a crown, and the purchaser of the balloon travelling the longest distance would receive two pounds. Balloon Races were very popular that year, I don't know if they still have them: you chose a pretty colour, and they tied a ticket on it with your name and address, and then everyone watched while you threw it up in the air and away it went on the wind. Mine was gold, at least yellow, but it looked gold when it soared and twisted and caught the sun . . . I could have written a poem about it, because I had one of those mysterious intuitions—I expect you have them sometimes, Mr. Chellyvah, you look as though you had!—a mysterious intuition that *my* balloon was bound to win and then I'd have the money to buy those cups and saucers; the organisers had to wait a few days, I forget how many, to get information from whoever picked them up to see which had travelled farthest."

"And in the end it was not yours? That was sad."

"I believe it *was* mine," Mrs. C. declared, revisited by passion; "yes, I still believe it; those intuitions of mine are never wrong when they're as strong as that, and Zillah Collier's balloon didn't go so very far, though farther than anybody else's except my gold one. Hers was green; I remember seeing her toss it lightly into the air. Naturally she didn't cheat or anything, she didn't even know about how I ached to have those cups and saucers on the shelf in my room because they reminded me of José and the happiest time of my life." . . . Mrs. C. gazed out across the flat expanse of Channel; the tide was coming in fast now, and the waves made a scalloped fringe along the beach as they curled gently to and fro, but she saw instead the steep cliffs of a little Cornish cove, the green water clear as glass merging into purple-black where the sea foamed round the rocks and threw up splinters of crystal spray. . . .

"Did you hear any more of your little gold balloon?" Adelbert inquired, recalling Mrs. C. with something of a start to the present moment.

"No, we never had any news of it. Perhaps it was carried along so far that it fell into the sea . . . or got caught in a tree of the forest, or some children found it and didn't bother to bring it back. The cups were bought by one of the summer visitors, a woman I couldn't bear, she was so rich and insolent; I do think life is full of coincidences, because she reminded me, just her looks and her insolence, of that bold Spanish-looking girl who took my José away. In a way Zillah Collier was more unselfish than me because she also spent her two pounds at Mr. Warren's shop, but on an old-fashioned musical box with tinkling tunes which she gave as a surprise to little Wendy Morrison though a musical box isn't exactly a child's toy, but that was Zillah all over, and of course we know she can't help exaggerating and making out she knows what people want better than they know themselves. And she doesn't always. Mr. Dymond teases her about how ridiculously she carries on as if she had a corner in 'wonderful intuitions,' but they didn't tell her how badly I wanted those cups and saucers from the same shop—the sort of thing one might have supposed *intuition* would have told about, just as mine told me that my balloon did go farther than hers."

Chapter Ten

SUSANNA REMAINED convalescent for some time; and convalescence brought its inevitable attendants of depression,
irritability and sheer indignant surprise that she should
have been selected to prove the literal truth of her
frequent remark that she simply didn't know the meaning
of illness. Though the disappearance of her naturally
sweet disposition was obviously only till she recovered her
physical health, it became apparent that those whom she
had hitherto loved most dearly had the power to exasperate
her most frequently; Geth rang up often from Whistle
Cottage to inquire, and could hardly believe it was his
mother replying to him with a list of nervous complications.
" Would you like to see me? " " Yes, darling, of course,
if you can bear such a tetchy old crock as I've become."
. . . But more than on either of her own daughters,
Bridget or Wendy, most of the nursing fell on Zillah,
giving Susanna hourly opportunities to observe and supply
ridiculous instances of the breakdown in the old Zillah
legend, which she called quite sincerely " the change in
Zillah " . . . never "the change in Susanna"; she would
wait till she had Bride or Geth or one of her nephews from
the Brown House up in her room, get rid of Zillah if she
were present, and then: " What *do* you think—? I could
hardly wait to tell you——" She thought the telling and
the subsequent laughter would be ointment to her frayed

nerves, and could not quite define why she should have the slight discomfort of feeling ashamed as well as diverted. Without bothering to work it out, she blamed the influenza bugs to begin with, then the late heat wave, and finally a plague of mosquitoes.

"——There it is *again*," cried Susanna, raising herself from the pillows piled behind her in the armchair and making ineffectual stabs at the air as a high whine pinged past her ear. "There it is again; the same one that kept me awake all last night."

"Darling, how can you know it's the same?"

"It *is* the same, Geth; I asked Zillah to kill it this morning while I was in the bathroom, and she didn't. It stung me *here* and *here* and in several other places I can't get at; look how they've swelled up." Everyone looked and commiserated. "As though one mosquito bite weren't enough to keep me awake and scratching and— On the ceiling, quick!"

Followed the chase and racket familiar to all those who have ever pitted their cunning against a mosquito in the room: furniture moved, hands suddenly clapped together, triumphant shouts of "*got* it!"—only to realise that after all they hadn't got it—till Zillah succeeded in slamming her palm square on that evil shape against the wall, and when she cautiously lifted it away, there it was, spread-eagled.

"You put murder into that punch of yours," Geth remarked, congratulating her.

"He might have kept Susanna awake all to-night as well."

"Do you always refer to a mosquito as *him*, not it?"

And as he had intended, off she went on her cue: "I understand its life and death better if I think of it as 'he,' and capable of enjoying a deep mouthful of me,

thinking ' she's delicious! ' and ' that was worth it! '
So it couldn't matter to him really if I dealt death right
on top of getting the taste and flavour of my red blood,
because he couldn't fear or feel death but could understand——''

" The taste and flavour of your red blood. What St.
Francis would have thought of you, my girl! "

" St. Francis would have been pleased with me,"
Zillah asserted. " I was the only one of you who
recognised that mosquito as Little Brother."

" St. Francis would have been more pleased with you
if you'd let it off. Or could you swear that you only hated
it on Susanna's account? "

Zillah squatted on the floor, hands clasped round her
knees, absorbed by this God-given—or Geth-given—
opportunity of making a passionate ass of herself. " When
I hate people I don't want to batter them with my fists
and make them suffer, and I don't feel as though I could
murder them; I just want them not to be there; *eliminate*,
that's the word—I want to *eliminate* them."

" But St. Francis," Geth went on tempting her to
further display of how hate and murder affected her,
"would he have wanted to 'eliminate' Brother Wolf?"
For her eyes had that intent, ecstatic look which he
recognised as a tie-up with some rarity she was about to
produce from her collection, more personally affiliated
than Brother Wolf. Nor was he disappointed.

" I forget the name of the little church; it was in the
West Country. I was wandering round by myself years
ago, and came across a statue of St. Francis in a niche in
an obscure corner; and I noticed a crumpled bit of paper
curled up at the edges tucked away half under the statue,
and I lifted it out, very carefully of course, and on it was
typed like a message left for me to pick up: ' of your

charity pray for the soul of Father Macnamara who died 17th September, 1943' . . . Wasn't it strange? "

" Why was it strange? " Geth asked.

A long pause. Then Zillah said lamely and on quite a different note, her temporary glow of exhilaration died down. " Because it was yesterday. To-day is the 18th."

" Every date is bound to have been yesterday if one mentions it to-day," Susanna interposed, half-asleep. " And if Zillah has finished babbling about her love-affairs with a mosquito, it's time I was back in bed. Geth, darling, you won't mind going now, will you? Richard will be coming up to me presently to say good night."

When Zillah had settled her patient for the night, she remembered she had a date with the Third Programme in about twenty minutes, and went into the deserted library to ponder sadly on the bleak landscape of her present existence, so altered that she felt now she would be less disconsolate alone, even without Heather; because Heather, forbidden to remind them about Zillah's birthday, was so furious with them all for forgetting it that one would rather not have to go on parrying her loyal questions: " Why don't you want them to know? It's over, and serve the beasts right to make them feel fed up with themselves! " . . . But as they *had* forgotten, any belated atonement hastily scrambled together in celebration would have a false note, and you couldn't bear that, while you still remembered the spontaneous fun and affection of every 17th September in the past. It was a premonition that it might work out like this which had inspired the sudden idea, when she saw the date on the poster announcing a day's trip to Brighton by coach, to arrange her own birthday treat not dependent on anyone remembering except herself. If they did recall it just beforehand, she could explain gaily, without any hurt undertones, that she and Mrs. C. were off to Brighton and no home festivities required, thank you. And if on the other hand they went on forgetting, the day would still have been different and special, to appease the childish part of you. But then Mrs. C. too had let you down. Or perhaps she hadn't? Perhaps she had genuinely taken for granted that in your capacity of nurse to Susanna, you would not have contemplated a day's outing? After all, to be fair, Mrs. C. hadn't known it was your birthday. . . . Yet all the same a let-down was implicitly contained in the way she took it for granted, with no lamentations nor attempts to try and find a substitute who would look after Mrs. Collier for just one day: " after all, you've had the brunt of it, and there's Mr. Collier and Ivy and Heather King; and Mrs. Collier isn't seriously ill any more."

So somehow you had had to get through yesterday as though it were any ordinary day; and there was a certain pride in that achievement; a lonely pride: nobody except yourself would ever know what it cost. And then just now you had again barely managed not to wreck it all by linking 17th September on to St. Francis, and in answer to Geth's " why was it strange? " flinging out " *because it was my birthday!* " And if that brought forth a burst of contrition, to have remarked with gentle dignity how birthdays and presents and treats were rather childish affairs and didn't really matter to you any more. . . .

It was still early, so as Bridget complained to Geth of not having seen him alone for more than a week, he didn't go straight home but stopped to have a whisky with her downstairs. So far, Bridget had shown herself the least obvious of their group in treating Zillah as a pearl of a joke; he was not prepared, therefore, for her to break out, without preliminaries, into a savage burlesque of Zillah's idiom and narrative style, and for a split second did not grasp whether this were not Bridget herself gone suddenly round the bend?

"——And *he* said that if he weren't an old man . . . so *I* said right away: ' but you're only half as old as time ' . . . I'd seen in his eyes when he looked at me so pathetically that he was longing to be contradicted, so of course I let him make love to me a bit; but then I simply couldn't keep back how 'half as old as time' might have been meant as just a matter-of-fact statement about the rose-red city because in John Burgon's days they thought the world had been created in 4004 B.C., which would make Petra 2,002 years old, which *would* be half as old as time and didn't he think that was madly, madly exciting, much more than the poetic part of it! ' and *he* said one didn't often come across a girl as beautiful as me who knew as much, instead of simply wanting to talk all the time about herself——"

" Here, hold on, Beryl; you're making up all that."

" Is it so ' out of character '? " Bride's dark sloe eyes danced in mockery.

" No, but it's a caricature."

" Caricature hell! I had it from her almost verbatim about ten days ago, and saved it up for you. Oh, I may have given it a shine where it's gone a little rusty, and I've a suspicion that the introduction ' If I weren't an old man, etc.' was invented on the spur of the moment to give herself a cue for sharing a bit of scholarship she'd grubbed up lately for her collection."

After a pause to assimilate the discovery that his sister had so far lapsed from adoration of Zillah as to leave them all nowhere, Geth remarked dryly: " You *have* brought pungency into the fruit salad, haven't you? "

" *You* have, and oh, God, was I grateful when you came home and set me free after two and a half years' bloody bondage! " She splashed an inch of soda into half a glass of neat whisky, drank it down, and took another, undiluted.

" When I heard you were on your way I dreaded having to watch you fall for all that bogus stuff, you too; I lay awake dreading it; you might even have married her, elder son making amends for the younger son, what could be more appropriate? And then we'd have to hear Zillah hand out some ballyhoo that it would have been Jackie's 'dearest wish'."

" Steady with the whisky, Beryl." Geth passed over her oblique reference to Jackie, to dwell on his awakened interest in John Burgon's rose-red city half as old as time: " I'd never heard that before; yes, he might have meant it literally; he was an orthodox churchman of the right period and it makes more solid sense than slamming it down for the sake of a beautiful metaphor."

But she rushed him past this typically Geth reaction; the barriers were down, the prison bars sawn through, she was released and she had to keep on in a spate of anti-Zillah: " Have you noticed how she can repeat her bogus effects for every fresh person who comes in, till she's worked that one out of her system? "

" That's the second time you've fixed ' bogus ' on to her; I'm inclined to think she isn't bogus in the sense of being a sham," Geth found himself oddly defending Zillah; " she can discriminate or she wouldn't have fished up the origin of a rose-red city to place among her curios." Bride made an impatient movement, but he continued his analysis: " Yes, but she discriminates at one remove, between the Right People to tell her what's really good in wine, acting, books, pictures, colours and so forth, yet not always between the things themselves; rose-red city might have been a lucky dip."

For Bridget, however, such abstract speculations held no kick; also by now she was far from sober; voice thickened, eyes and ears obstinately, truculently rejecting everything which did not bear on her obsession: " Mother's wise to her; she began to be before she got 'flu, and now Zillah drives her up the wall; the only relief she can get is in talking her over with us afterwards. Nice change in Mother; I used to have to watch her Seeing the Best in Zillah till I could have screamed. . . . It was her birthday yesterday," Bridget added casually; " no, not Mother's, Zillah's. You couldn't have known, of course. She's improving, isn't she? Everybody forgetting about it was almost more than she could bear, but she just managed to get through the day without reminding us."

" *Everybody* forgetting? You too, until just now? "

" Oh, no, I remembered right enough; it amused me to watch Zillah holding herself back all day. And she had another Herculean struggle to-night not to blow the gaff: ' I forget the name of the church; I was wandering round and came across a statue of St. Francis, and what *do* you think!—a crumpled bit of paper was tucked away under it, and I drew it out, and on it was typed like a message for me: " In charity pray for the soul of Father Cascara who died 17th September nineteen forty-something "— Wasn't it *strange*? ' "

. . . After a moment's silence, Geth remarked: " I'd no idea you were such a brilliant mimic. You should have taken up acting as a career when you came home from Malaya."

And now what gnawed at the root of her bitter antagonism remained no longer hidden: "Zillah discouraged me at the psychological moment; she threw all her enthusiasm into discouraging me; I desperately wanted to go on the stage, and then Zillah narrowed her eyes and scrutinised me and swept away every scrap of belief in myself; she said she had an instinct for these things, and she'd heard me burlesquing a story to some visitors, and I'd been so determined to put it across that I'd ruined it by overacting. Great fun to hear that, as you can imagine! Darling little Zillah's so sensitive over our most vulnerable spot; there lay my vanity slain on the ground . . .' but you've got it in you to be a wonderful organiser,' consoling the corpse. ' Don't you worry, Bride, I swear I'll get you fixed up! ' . . . So she *got* me fixed up: house-agenting and an antique shop and never an idle moment! Bridget Ogilvie is known for miles around as a *wonderful* organiser."

" Look, Beryl, what made you take any notice? You've never been a weak character, and Zillah was years younger than you."

" That was it: her youthful energy pouring in, and I'd made an outsize flop of my marriage, and when you're already a failure you dare not risk another mistake so soon, make a public fool of yourself. And believing in myself as an actress would have been such a juvenile delusion; I couldn't be *sure*, with Zillah's eyes on me all the time——"

" Yet you yourself bolstered up the Zillah legend."

" *Never!* Faked it."

" Then why didn't you break right away instead? Live somewhere else? "

" Oh, lack of money, and a job found for me here— this was my home, after all. And besides, Max being in the neighbourhood——"

Again for an instant Geth wondered if he had gone mad and if his sister had turned into Zillah before his very eyes, throwing in an unidentified name and not caring whether he recognised " Max " in any man he had met since his

133

return? But before he could decide, Bride explained curtly: "Max lives near Oldbridge so never mind his surname; he's married and won't ask for a divorce; suppose Zillah got hold of that, *think* what she'd do and wouldn't do to help us 'face up to it' and wreck the whole shoot! Zillah's all for 'facing up to it.' Look at Wendy and her career. . . . That's why Wendy went off with the O'Gradys; she doesn't much care for Barbara O'Grady, but she'd had enough of career this and career that and being started early into something she'd love and would suit her and which Zillah would find for her—' It's important, for you of all people!'"

"How did you know Wendy was feeling like that?"

"Told me herself. When you and I were last in England just before Mother met and married Richard, Jackie sort of belonged to you and Wendy to me; she wasn't seven yet; and when I turned up next time, she couldn't have cared less about me; Zillah had annexed her. You don't believe in showing your hand, Geth dear, but accept my thanks on behalf of a grateful family. . . . D'you remember how at the Czelovar's house-warming when Zillah came in with her 'Robbikins' and said Robert as a name was 'too solid and worthy for me to live up to'? Robert Lee-Curtis couldn't make out why we all laughed so long and loud and impolitely . . . till I told him, and then he laughed too and thought it damn' funny. He'll have spread it over the whole neighbourhood of Long Swynton by now."

"Did you have to enlighten the young man?"

"Oh, he dropped into the shop a few days later to get his mother a birthday present; she fancied a tea-caddy and I had rather a good one. . . .No, I didn't *have* to tell him, I chose to."

"I'm off," said Geth for the second time; wondering

why he need have been more shocked by her stark hate of Zillah as revealed in this minor incident, than in all that had gone before.

Bridget hardly noticed him depart; her mind, clearer for a moment, stumbled, and slipped again into a drunken sprawl; she had reached that stage when she could just as well chew alone over her grouch; nor did she perceive her brother's temporary withdrawal from an alliance that he himself had certainly, though not openly, brought into being.

Passing the library door on his way out, Geth was surprised to hear the radio loudly turned on. And pausing to listen, it seemed to announce that the subject was *bulbs*. Strange! Only Susanna in that household was interested. in gardening. The door was a little ajar; he pushed it open farther, and stood silently on the threshold . . . looking at Zillah who squatted on the floor beside the wireless set, her hair falling over her face, concentrated, absorbed, a block and pencil in her hand to scribble down at a feverish rate as much as she could get of a man's voice reading aloud or reciting. Geth was inclined to reconsider his first careless assumption that the speaker was a professional gardener; bulbs certainly came into it, but this was poetry and good poetry too, exotic in substance despite the deliberately matter-of-fact voice. But what was Zillah up to now, squatting there by herself on the rug close beside the radio . . . so forlorn that had she still been a child in years, he might have offered to give her a puppy.

(. . . "Anyone becomes important by being desperately unhappy.")

The programme came to an end, and she switched off. Geth made a movement and she started, looked round and saw him, and for a wonder did not put on an act but

merely said: " Wasn't it lovely?   Did you hear it all? "
" No, what was it? Third Programme, I imagine? "
" Yes; Sacheverell Sitwell reading from his series of
unpublished poems based on the names of Dutch hyacinths
in an old catalogue. And they were *fabulous*! I happened
to come in on it before the News when he first did it, and
then luckily I saw there was a repeat to-night. I thought
you'd gone home."
" I'm going now. Good night."

. . . Trying feverishly to catch the freaks of a poet's
imagination and get them written down; nothing per-
plexing about it, once you knew the way Zillah functioned:
she was replenishing her stock-in-trade, lately im-
poverished.

All the same, driving back to Whistle Cottage along
the quiet roads, he wondered why this glimpse of her
should have touched him to compunction. And con-
cluded that Beryl was responsible by her zeal in telling
Robert Lee-Curtis why all of them were laughing at
Zillah's unabashed variations on her first name, her
nickname, her real name; and, a further refinement of
cruelty, all day yesterday watching her struggle not to
mention that it was her birthday.

He hoped this mood would soon pass; compunction,
thank God, wasn't part of *his* stock-in-trade.

Chapter Eleven

MORE AND more urgently in need of reassurance, Zillah
tried to persuade herself that it was all imagination, these
cool airs and draughts that blew on her whenever she
tried out all her previous gay little tricks and successes:
they *did* work but not in the right way, and she was unable
to break through the change, spin it back widdershins into
the past, sun herself and bask as she had done before last
summer, before Geth came back. And yet in her present
desolation she told herself that of her whole circle of
family and friends, of the whole body of membership
(though they did not feature verbally in this guise) only
Geth was still nice to her.

A sudden change . . . and noticing that Zillah was
mysteriously drawing on some inward source of happiness,
Geth wondered whence it came. Yet though apparently
confidence was flowing back like an incoming tide from
the horizon, she was gentler than she had been on their
first encounter; nor were her stories as fantastic as when
she had still tried to believe she could win back what was
lost by using everything she had and more. Yes, Zillah
debonair again; and no longer dependent on putting
herself across as though life and breath depended on it.
And next, a new name recurring in her chronicles; one
name, Edward, in lieu of a scatter of Peters and Johns and

Michaels. Edward. No surname, of course! And here and there other names naturally attaching themselves to this Edward as might be of his relations or his friends. Without doubt, then, here was a conquest, a victim, the prince of the fairy-tale, the boy-friend to end all boy-friends. And when he heard her allude casually to an unalarming future as "until I marry" instead of "unless I marry," indicating that all this adoption business they had heard so much about had been only a substitute for what she had really wanted and needed all the time, he felt he was justified in asking Susanna: "Who *is* this Edward? And where's Zillah?"

His mother could hardly believe that Geth was not in full possession of the facts. "You'd have heard all about it at our dinner party the day before yesterday."

"Wasn't asked."

"Oh, Geth, of course you were; you're asked to all our dinner parties; they wouldn't be——"

"——complete without me. But I still don't know about this Edward of Zillah's. Has he got a surname? Profession? Serious intentions?"

"Zillah's gone up to London to stay with his people."

"Quick work! That does sound like 'serious intentions'."

"Oh, yes, at any moment we're expecting to hear they're engaged."

Geth lifted a quizzical eyebrow and waited. Susanna was never garrulous, so he would not have to sift through a mass of irrelevant details before she put him in possession of the facts relating to an impending stepbrother-in-law of unimpeachable eligibility: Edward Saxton, Foreign Service; only son of Sir William Saxton, Bt.; permanent residence, when in England, his parents' flat in London. His previous assignment had been Vienna, and now he

was appointed First Secretary and Consul to Montevideo. " We think that if he intends to marry Zillah, and
I'm sure he does, it will have to be almost at once so that
he can take her out with him; and he has only four or
five weeks left of his leave, because the Ambassador needs
him as soon as possible so that he himself can go to Punta
del Este for the summer, that's our winter but terribly hot
out there. And Richard says they'd have to be inoculated
first."

" I see. You'll miss her, won't you? "

" Naturally we'd all miss her, but——" Susanna
hesitated, not quite able to explain that Zillah's going so
far away need not now be something she dreaded as she
had years ago when there were still difficult children in
the house, Jackie and Wendy, whom she could hand over,
lock, stock and barrel.

" Where did she meet him? "

" Geth, dear, I *must* have told you that! " But then it
transpired that here was a gap left from Zillah's old
repertory style: a name had blossomed in the foliage . . .
and as she had not worked up an exciting story, their
meeting had probably been quite undramatically at someone's cocktail party—" in fact, it must have been at or
through the Czelovars because they knew about him from
when he was at the Embassy in Vienna; or perhaps
Adelbert said that when he went to Vienna last year to
see his cousins, he had met him there. He isn't a young
man any more, about thirty-eight or thirty-nine; just
right for Zillah "—the implication that Jackie had been
far too young, was not actually spoken.

" Has he been married before? Thirty-nine years is a
long time to have remained unattached on the off-chance
of Zillah turning up in his life? "

" No, Adelbert said there had been a beautiful married

woman, a sort of discreet permanent affair—and then he went tiresomely secretive. It's essential, of course, that nothing should filter through when you're Foreign Service. She died, so that's all right."

"Quite all right," Geth assented.

"The title will come to him; he's the last male of his family so they're anxious it shouldn't become extinct. You remember how Zillah has always said she'd like to adopt lots and lots of children, but in her heart I expect she'd prefer real ones——" Geth smiled at "real ones" and agreed; glad that his mother should be so perfectly at ease with him. "I'm not sure whether I ought to be telling you all this before they're officially engaged."

"I'm not sure either, Mother dear, but it's done now, and it certainly sounds as though they were on the brink of it. What's he like to look at, this incredibly right-for-Zillah man?"

Into Susanna's voice, perennially youthful, came that sparkle which one associates with a young girl in raptures over her favourite film star. "He's like—well, he's not good-looking in the strict sense, not as good-looking as Gregory Peck but more like Gary Cooper—Geth, what are you laughing at?"

"Nothing, dear. Go on."

"He's tall and very dark, one of those lean, irregular faces, ugly-handsome, and a long strong chin that you can lean on—*Geth!*"

"I wasn't laughing," her son pleaded untruthfully.

"I'm only trying to give you an idea."

"You are. I apologise. Do go on. But if that's how you feel, please convey to Richard my profound apprehension for his peace of mind! And let me know when the engagement is official."

And a few days later she rang up to tell him that a

radiantly happy Zillah had just returned from her visit to London, and the engagement *was* official. " And I've had a letter from his mother, she sounds a dear, and she says they're prepared to give such a sweet little daughter-in-law the warmest of welcomes, and if I don't mind, they'll have the wedding from their house . . . so much easier for all their friends in London." Understandable that Cobblers Meadow had this touch-wood feeling about the wedding ceremony. " And Richard says better a mature man who would stand no nonsense than a mere lad."

Woebegone at the prospect of Zillah going so far away from England for years and years, Heather could not but be exultant that her heroine had been so gloriously vindicated: " And she promised I should come and stay with her out in South America; another continent, think what bliss! And of course she'll write us long letters."

" Yes, I could almost write them beforehand except for the local flora and fauna."

" Bridget, what *do* you mean? " from a mystified Heather. Though it was never easy to impress Bridget. But Wendy, just returned from her stay with the O'Gradys, was young enough to be awed by the high-class standard of Zillah's engagement, and rather hoped that her cousin Heather would not remind her too often of her anti-Zillah period. Which of course Heather did.

Bridget's reaction to the news had been mixed: reluctant as she was to admit that the fun was over, of plugging Zillah as a pearl of a joke, an unspoken " wait for it! " on her every entrance, at least the panic was also over that Geth might fall for Zillah as had the rest of the family (" I suppose this Edward first saw her looking like a crushed snowdrop, and that helped to bring it on.")

But the prospective wedding had swung her out of reach as an effective target for taunts, so Bride turned back once more to Mrs. C., who found them harder to bear after her period of immunity than when she could have expected them at any moment and all the time. She'll go too far, thought Mrs. C., and I don't see why I should stand for it next time she insults me in front of people—"I shouldn't mind so much if we were alone," for since that day with Adelbert at Brighton, it may have been the sea air, her spirit of independence had gained strength.

Meanwhile she mused on what to give Zillah as a wedding present? " I know what she'd like; something *personal*. They're bound to get some very handsome gifts from all the Diplomatic set they hobnob with, and of course I can't afford to compete, but it's the personal touch that always counts—you can see at once if someone has given the matter real thought. And another thing, it mustn't be anything bulky because of taking it with her out to South America; silly to choose something which would lie in store for years until she had a home of her own in England! " Something small, therefore. And with that, came the inspiration she was waiting for: a rather seedy artist had come to live in the neighbourhood and had brought along some of his stuff to Bridget's antique shop in the hope she would give it a permanent place in the window and obtain commissions for him. Mrs. Bride, however, had been much too brisk with him and sent him to the right-about with as little compassion, thought Mrs. C., as if he'd been a *hawker*; and this was all the more upsetting, because the first time he had called, Mrs. C. was alone in the shop and had encouraged him—" artists need encouragement; besides, he's worth it. Mrs. Bride is apt to mistake delicate execution for weakness; I dare say if he'd produced some of those

dreadfully bold Post-Impressionist daubs instead——"
And delicate work suggested—what? Why, miniatures,
of course! A miniature of either Zillah or Edward, and
whichever they preferred could give it to the other.
Unluckily, however, for the encouragement of Mr. Adrian
Pettifer, a miniature, he said, would require at least ten
sittings, and neither Zillah nor Edward could spare
leisure to " sit " in the crowded days ahead. Zillah broke
this to Mrs. C. as nicely as possible: " You see, there are
all my clothes to get ready for a boiling hot climate—it's
their summer when it's our winter, but of course you knew
that, and the sea voyage takes three weeks and that will
have to be our honeymoon; we can't fly—it would be
much quicker but then the Government wouldn't pay
our fares, and our passages are already booked. I'd *adore*
a miniature of Edward if only there'd been time, and it
was really very, very sweet of you to have such an original
idea! "

Still determined to encourage her artist and at the same
time to give Zillah a romantic present which would stand
out from the conventional array of silver, glass and china,
Mrs. C. triumphantly commissioned a painting of Cobblers
Meadow—" Not on a large canvas; I believe there's
something in the Customs about taking out works of art
to foreign places, they have to be either over or under a
hundred years old, and then they do or don't become
antiques. Not that Mr. Saxton would mind paying duty,
but we must be practical. I think, don't you, a view of
the house which would bring in her own bedroom window,
not dragging it in, but as though that were the natural
place for you just to happen to set up your easel to paint it
from." So there Mr. Pettifer sat day after day with his
easel outside Cobblers Meadow, in the most natural place
for bringing in Zillah's window and also for getting in the

way of all vehicles as they drove in and out. " And every time she's homesick out there, I can guess what it will *mean* to her sensitive nature. . . ." Thus Mrs. C. worked out of her system a buried uneasiness that once, not so long ago and in the wish to remain in on the popular side, she may have let down this very Zillah to whom she now attributed the same sensitive nostalgia which had caused Mrs. C. to hanker for a cup and saucer with a view of the Cornish harbour where she herself as a girl had walked in bliss with José before that dark unscrupulous woman had snatched him from her. . . . " I do so hope Zillah will be careful to keep that type away from her husband, though difficult to keep anyone away as our Ambassador's a bachelor and she says, or Mr. Edward says, she'll be entertaining at the Embassy as his wife and that means being amiable to everybody. Of course everyone can see that he's frightfully in love with her now, but we don't know, do we, if Zillah can *hold* a man? "

" Our Mrs. C. has had an equally artistic idea!"— Bridget flung the mocking compliment across the shop at her assistant, when Adelbert Czelovar, after consultation with Richard, came in one morning in quest of a Baxter print as a wedding present to Zillah and Edward which would remind them, in South America, of a typical English scene and weather. " But *she* fancies herself as Patron of the Arts and of the living artist. Or might it be that our Mrs. C. has let herself be blinded by the dashing good looks of Mr. Adrian Pettifer? I expect you've nearly fallen over him and his easel every time you've been up to Cobblers Meadow lately? "

A pearl of a joke; but Adelbert merely said that he was sure the young couple would appreciate a picture of Cobblers Meadow, and went on poring over the Baxters.

The last straw! Mrs. C. had told herself that when it did happen, she would hand in her notice. And handed it in.

The Czelovars were perhaps hardly quite competent to give linguistic aid in drawing up an advertisement for another job, but they were interested and kind, and Mrs. C. looked on them as her friends. So, two or three days later, she trotted over to Jake's Parcel and read aloud a rough draft of what she had already prepared: " *Experienced Lady, reliable, not afraid of hard work, requires post near Oldbridge*—because I don't want to go too far away from all my friends—*fifteen years head clerk in house-agents' office who would give excellent references*—that would be Mr. Collier and Mr. Barry King—*subsequently*—oh dear, that's a very long word and might put people off but there isn't another—*subsequently six years as assistant manageress in a high-class antique-shop*—I was going to mention my exact age, but perhaps if I just insert *no longer in her first youth* straight after *Experienced Lady*——? "

Erda was home for the week-end, and as she had been told to switch off the radio, listened instead to this curious conversation going on above her head. " How old is *no longer in her first youth*? " she interrupted. " When does it end and one's second youth begin? Am *I* in my first youth? And you, Grandmama, are you no longer in your first youth? "

After the Czelovars had whittled down Mrs. C.'s advertisement to a length which allowed coherence but eliminated extravagance, and following her departure full of gratitude for their sympathy—" We are neither of us in our first youth, you and I, Mama, only you do not enough spare yourself," Adelbert informed his mother. " When you cook, when you make pastry, when you wish to give us your *Powidl* and *Apfelstrudel* and *Schlusselbuben*, *es ist immer mit Herzen gemacht,* and afterwards, though you do not confess it, you look tired." Whereupon he went on to suggest that they should offer Mrs. C. a job with them as companion-cook-housekeeper-and-head-bottle-washer, using, however, any inclusive name that would not let her feel she had come down in the world. For " come down in the world" had also been a phrase that puzzled and charmed Erda when Mrs. C. had used it in pouring out her story. " I don't want Mrs. Bride to think I've come down in the world, so it's no use drawing up an ad. that would bring in a lot of letters from the wrong sort of people, is it? "

Elisabeta Czelovar did not contest his offer of Mrs. C.'s support in the household as vigorously as he had expected. She *had* been feeling tired lately, and their daily, Mrs. Button, was an uncertain quantity. So she merely stipulated: " She vill not live inside vis us? "

" *Nein, nein,* she has her own bedroom at the Brown House, and here, too, the small Eastern room which we never enter can be her sitting-room, and I will put up a shelf for her blue cups and saucers."

" Has she then so many? "

Adelbert Czelovar smiled and did not explain.

" Papa, you shouldn't say *Eastern* room," cried pert little Erda, glad of the opportunity to correct his English, for as they had wished her to become fluent in her adopted language she had been forbidden to lapse into her native tongue and they never spoke German together when she was present; " you should say the small *East* room, Papa. I know, because at Marian's when to tea in her house, they have a West Room, do you understand, not *Western*? "

" That will be the afternoon post." Not deigning any further reply, her father went into the hall to fetch the letters.

" This is for both of us," said his mother after reading
it; " from Zillah Collier, so sweet she writes and so
pleased viz her picture from us." She passed the letter
over to her son to read, and went on: " *Sag' nun mal,*
Adelbert, I have vundered, do you think zat Geth Dymond
vas in love with her and is now broken-heart? "

" I do not think so, no, Mama, but you could ask him,
if you take care when you do that you have not his deaf
ear."

" But if he fell in love viz her when he came back from
abroad, why zen did he not speak at once and not hang
in the fire till your friend Edward Saxton cuts first? "

" Erda, to bed! " Again they had forgotten she was in
the room.

" High-time, too! " When it came to English idiom,
Erda had the last word.

So the engagement was not just a phantasmagoria of
Zillah's imagination; and Geth thought: " Where do we
go from here? " Whatever he might feel he had to do to
prevent this marriage would have to be rapid. When he
returned to his family last spring after eight years of
absence, he had deliberately intended, for Jackie's
justification in their eyes, to strip her of the uncritical
worship she had somehow evoked in presenting the Zillah-
legend; they were not intelligent over character (except
Bridget, whom he latterly reckoned as the only bad nature
among them) and though truthful, knew very little about
truth; his repudiation of the way Zillah constantly violated
integrity, would have wholly mystified them; he had had
to expose her gradually by ridicule, and this had been
achieved; nor did he say to himself that Jackie could lie
quiet now, because he was an unbeliever of " now " in
terms of the Hereafter; though granted you had to define

and then abide by the verdict of "mind your own business," it *had* been his business to protect Jackie's kindred, avert future damage by Zillah. But was he to consider it equally his business, or rather his serious duty, to see Edward Saxton and somehow put him wise? That must depend on whether the man proved to be a type who could look after himself. "If he is, I'm let off any responsibility." A word with Adelbert Czelovar might come in useful; then a few days in London on an unassailable reason connected with his own book; one's publishers could always be trusted to provide an unassailable reason; then get in touch with Edward, introduce himself as Susanna Collier's son, and ask as a favour if they could meet for lunch at his Club, because he had heard that the other would very shortly be off to Uruguay and there were two or three questions Geth would like answered which could only proceed from information gathered on the spot by someone with special facilities. Edward Saxton would probably often be seeing one or other of the Military Attachés when they came over from Buenos Aires, who might be able to check up on an expedition in 1953 for investigating the remains of the Jesuit communities in Paraguay, and ascertain in what condition they were keeping the church in Caapucú. A foolproof excuse for the encounter, because he knew that Professor Buré, who had led their party, would be glad to obtain their information through confidential channels; and half an hour alone with Zillah's fiancé, less than half an hour, must show Geth whether or not he had to force a showdown; but it had to be alone, not in a family circle with Zillah dancing around and doing a " me too " on the slightest provocation, as when Richard had suggested a man-to-man session in his study, and Zillah, unable to see what was wrong with " me too," had to be quite brutally rebuffed by her father; if Edward were so deeply in love and not capable of Richard's firmness, " me too " would have its way. So nothing else for it; it had to be London and the Club.

And he returned satisfied; by his impression of Edward Saxton absolved from any duty of putting him wise to what he was in for; as he had said, mere revenge was not his business, and this man *could* look after himself.

A moment he had hesitated, contemplating the fate of Zillah's children, " lots and lots of children," a primitive need probably at the root of all her rapacious desire for notice; there was so much of Zillah that she longed to extend in her own flesh and blood the energy hitherto gone into the creation of all these castellated turrets and minarets and castles-in-the-ego. And though people who were not attracted by her might say in vicarious com-miseration, " Sorry for her children," these putative children would certainly be loved tenderly and must take their chance of her over-possessive maternal instinct, as other unborn children had to take their chance of a parent neglectful and unloving; you could not arrange before-hand for such extreme natures to be barren.

Geth wondered, not for the first time, what Zillah's mother had been like. And wished, quite for the first time, that Richard Collier on this theme had had less of his admirable quality of reticence. Perhaps Zillah's " lots and lots of children " would have enough of Zillah in them to stand up to her, help their weaker brothers and sisters to escape; or it might be some of them would not even want to fulfil themselves by escape. Or perhaps in the reality of actually giving birth at last, she would learn a modicum of expedience—or at any rate, tire herself out for the next twenty years or so.

So let it all ride.

Chapter Twelve

ZILLAH'S REVERIE was too blissful to let her be aware of
the bus lurching and bumping along the road in the
streaming rain, on her way to see Geth at Whistle Cottage.
She had returned that morning to Cobblers Meadow from
her second stay with Edward's people, and their wedding
was to be so soon that the next fortnight already had that
breathless gone-with-the-wind look: "Thursday—Friday
—Monday—and we haven't done a thing yet!" Not
only the wedding itself, but preparations had to be made
for going abroad to another continent and not returning
for three years; never mind, homesickness could not
exist where Edward would be. Oh, thank God for
Edward, and for Edward falling in love with her, and for
no delays nor problems to be solved before she could
become his wife! And thank God for their children so
nearly existing in substance instead of in images fancifully
conceived to delude herself and others and fill up that shame-
ful void since Jackie had deserted her at the very altar.
She simply could not understand why from then onwards
all her suitors had somehow in one way or another escaped
from her. Yet they had been crazy for her at first . . .
those golden extravagant ways of describing her, she *had*
to repeat them afterwards to everyone, she couldn't help
it, how were people to know otherwise that they had been
said about this very Zillah?

" I am on fire with that sweet sound
You make in uttering my name "—

—so David had murmured, David the only man until
Edward who had really counted (for Jackie had been still
a boy). And Edward never thought of things like that;
you simply couldn't begin to imagine him *quoting* while
he was making love; in fact, he didn't " make " love at
all, he——

—Bus-stop; no one to get out and no one got in.
Luckily the conductor seemed a taciturn man, rather like
Daddy. Never again would you need to rush into talk
with any man, caring nothing for his surprise (" Can you
turn a cartwheel? Oh, I often do; just limbering up; it's
easy! ")

Have I ever turned a cartwheel for Edward? No, I
don't believe I have, and if I asked: " Can *you* do it? "
Softly she laughed, imagining his grave answer: " No,
but in my profession it's possible to manage without";
not " Do show me how " or " I couldn't in a hundred
years " or any other superfluous assurance that her cheap
facility was wonderful and unique. You didn't perform
for Edward, nor talk wildly as to all the others; you didn't
have to; though you needn't always be relevant, either.
How had the subject come up yesterday, for instance, of
grown-ups so often not understanding what went on in a
child's mind?—" spoiling them is miles away from *understanding*. I once had a ticket for the Balloon Race at our
Village Fête, and the prize was two pounds, so on the off-
chance of winning it, I asked Jackie and Wendy what
they would choose if they were granted a wish. And of
all extraordinary things for an eight-year-old to wish for,
Wendy said an organ! Of course I didn't laugh at her nor
ask if she also wished for a church to go round it, and my

balloon *did* win, and at the antique shop they had a delicious little musical box, one of the old-fashioned kind with a picture on the lid, and you turned a handle and it tinkled out its tiny repertoire; old Mr. Warren—he kept the shop then—had a thing about me, so he let me have it for two pounds, and you should have *seen* Wendy's face when I gave it to her and asked would it do instead of an organ. Simply thrilled to the bone!"

"Was she? When I was a kid, I believe I'd have preferred a barrel-organ."

"Edward, darling you were a little *boy*; little girls are different; we don't always——"

Interrupted by Lady Saxton with visitors! Visitors, when you and he wanted to be left alone! Though good practice for Montevideo, putting up with duds. And they stayed and stayed as duds always do; and when at last they left, Edward remarked: "One can say to people who are late ' I thought you were never coming,' but not ' I thought you were never going' " . . . and took her in his arms.

"Sorry you've had this long wait, miss; one of the plugs; we had to call up the depot for a replacement."

Zillah started; she hadn't even noticed they had stopped for about twenty minutes, and only now were lurching on again. Still quite a distance from here to Whistle Cottage; perhaps she had been an ass to come? Never mind, it wasn't late, and probably Geth would run her back in his car when she had had the satisfaction of hearing him praise Edward. She hardly bothered to wonder why Geth had sought contact with him, phoned and invited him to lunch at his Club. . . . Zillah smiled at a mischievous image thus called up, of two males in a corner of the dining-room absorbed in a conversation strictly relevant to the subject in hand, no digressions. Edward had mentioned afterwards casually: " He wanted to ask if I could check up on conditions in Paraguay since he'd been out there with a party investigating what had remained of the Jesuit communities." Had she known beforehand, she would have exclaimed: " I'm coming too," and then there *would* have been digressions. . . . " Yes," Edward assented, " that's why I didn't tell you beforehand." " But, Edward, I'd have been madly interested in Jesuit communities—you know I'm interested in everything." " I do know, darling, and you are; only at any moment you might have gone off at a tangent about—well, about your Grannie's muff"—And you had to acknowledge the justice of this. She had brought up that faded photo of Grannie as a young woman to show him, because Grannie had said she looked rather like her at that stage. You could just remember Grannie elaborately dressed for a drive round the Park. " Oh, how beautiful you look! Let me hold your muff just for a moment; let me smell it," snuggling her face deeper into the chinchilla and savouring the faraway perfume that clung about the silken orchids laid in a trail across the fur. " Take care, Zillah dear, you're pulling at the chain." The chain was silver set with semi-precious stones, but Grannie, an Edwardian flirt, said that when they were young, she and her friends, they preferred a muff to be without a chain, holding it high up in front of the face to peep over the top as a provocative signal to some infatuated admirer to come across, and then dropping it on purpose to have it gallantly retrieved—"Or we'd carry it with *élan* to help us make an entrance into the room with a rival watching." " But, Grannie, didn't you ever use your muff to keep your fingers warm? "

In the lives girls led nowadays, fat lot of chance to snuggle icy fingers deep into the protective warmth of the dove-grey velvet lining!—"Fun to have a muff to do all those things with! " And looking over her shoulder at the photo, Edward promised to give her one exactly like it— " so useful in tropical climates."

" Oh, Edward, *darling*, you must always take what I say with a grain of salt."

" I know; I'm laying in a stock of salt."

. . . None of this counted; what counted was Edward himself; Edward who never threw his weight about, never boasted but rested every question on a deep assured basis of male arrogance; and now and then came out with a sardonic twist that turned all her bones to water. . . . Her joy in him could not fluctuate as it had done with Michael or Tommy or John or Brian or the other Michael. Curious, in some ways he reminded you more of Geth than of anyone, except that although Geth had that pleasant voice seeming to disinherit all serious meaning even while what he was saying had a serious significance, he wasn't at all attractive in the subconscious way—no, in the *un*conscious way, Edward hadn't a subconscious!—which everybody acknowledged in her future husband. Men liked Edward for one sort of reason, women for another; men because he was so down-to-earth and reasonable and masculine, and women because he was so poised and attractive—and masculine. A foregone conclusion what Geth would have thought of him, but when you're in love, proudly and happily in love, you like to hear voices actually saying what you're already aware they're going to say.

Till she sighted the tall poplar standing beside the road at the nearest point to Whistle Cottage, each landmark was calling up associations with her lonely childhood after Grannie died. Nannie had been a vigilant guardian of her physical welfare, but otherwise thought that listening to a waterfall of chatter and giving intelligent replies formed no part of her duties. And as for Daddy, he could hardly wait until you were old enough for boarding-school, hardly conceal his dismay at the length of the holidays. ... Until that evening when everything had changed, and her *darling* new family, Susanna, Wendy, Jackie, had come to stay for the week-end. And Daddy had married Susanna and they had all moved over to live at Cobblers Meadow. And that was the end of Whistle Cottage, till Geth's return from abroad. ...

"Whistle Cottage, miss," the bus had jerked to a halt. "Brought a torch? It's raining cats and dogs and I don't see no light across the fields."

"No, it's all right, his window faces the other way. But I used to live here, so I know every inch of the path. Thank you very much. Good night." She leapt from the step into a large puddle and waved to the departing bus conductor; wrapped round her head one of the "millions of different scarves" she found rammed down in her pocket, wondered again for an instant if she had been too impetuous in coming over without first ringing up Geth; then remembered that the telephone was upstairs in his bedroom and that he worked not in the main part of the cottage but in that little panelled room at the far end which he had taken for his study, so if she had stopped to phone and perhaps missed the bus going that way, he would probably still not have heard; authors like to isolate themselves from noise and interruption, and Geth's deaf ear was in this respect rather an advantage to him, though his hearing in the other ear was perfectly good when you were on his left side. Not enamoured of the idea of knocking in vain while she stood in the deluge at the front door, she took a short-cut through the sodden garden and round to the back. Yes, there was a light upstairs; he hadn't drawn the curtains across the window; Zillah stood below and called "Geth!" and then louder,

" 'Hoy, *Ge-eth*! " . . . supplying him with a fanciful selection of answers from Shakespeare. " What angel calls me from my flowery bed? " or " How cam'st thou hither, tell me, and wherefore? " . . . But Geth flung open the window, and called down an impatient: " Who the hell's there? "

" Me. Zillah."

A pause. Then: " O.K. I suppose you'd better come in. The door isn't locked."

" What a glowing welcome," she laughed, not a whit crushed. And when he came down, he found her making herself at home in the front sitting-room, flung down in an armchair and luxuriating in the warmth of the electric fire she had switched on.

" What d'you want, young woman? Can't you stay in your own home when you're only just back from London? "

" This *was* my own home." She kicked off her sandals, gay and impenitent. " My feet are *sopping*."

" Well, if you will come out in those gossamer affairs on a night like this——" Irritably, he propped them up to dry.

"Yes, it was idiotic; but I only had a moment to catch the bus, so I rushed out just as I was. Do sit down, Geth," for he stood over her, seeming reluctant to abandon all idea of returning to his desk and his manuscripts; " don't go on being a disgruntled author; sit down and let's be comfortable, and now you've met him, tell me what you think of Edward."

" What I think of Edward? " slowly. " I think you're in luck, Zillah." Then he could have kicked himself for giving her this opening for a merry: " And don't you think he's in luck too? " He could almost hear Bridget saying, " Wait for it! "

But she replied humbly: " Yes, I know I am"; and, a little ashamed of his surly response, Geth said: " I'll get you a drink," disregarding her protest that she didn't want it. " Or—yes, I'd better have one; let's take every precaution against a cold in the head for one's wedding day! "

So Zillah had come over not only to talk about Edward and hear him praise Edward; Geth felt that Edward plus wedding day was going to be more than he could stand. . . . He went off into the dining-room, once more afraid of his own mood.

When he returned, he found Zillah happily singing a little off the key:

> *Every afternoon at three*
> *Jolly little Polly on her gee-gee-gee*

(Come now, this was more favourable; the words appeared to have no connection with Edward or lovers or wedding days.)

> *Trotting along in front of me,*
> *Hasn't got a little bit of pedigree—*

"That was one of Grannie's songs. The Negroes on the sands at Broadstairs sang it, she said, when she was a little girl, and she and the other children used to shout the chorus while they were taken for donkey rides; I wondered for years what 'pedigree' meant—I thought it must be something like a carrot or a lump of sugar and the donkey hadn't got even a little bit of it. I must show you a photo I've got of Grannie as a young girl: she was deliciously pretty, but Edward said——"

Zillah stopped. How funny, she had no desire, after all, to repeat to Geth nor to anybody else her satisfaction in the almost disparaging things Edward let fall: " You're not half as pretty as your Grannie, but for keeps I'd rather have you "—you could just relax, letting it begin and end with Edward with whom everything was different . . . so different it was all going to be this time. And she went on musing aloud: " I'd ask you instead of Daddy to give me away, only I suppose it would look queer to Edward's parents, with Daddy still alive and on the spot."

" No, Zillah, I won't give you away." Geth's inflection —was it her fancy?—wasn't on its usual light note of chaffing her, making a joke of her nonsense, never taking her seriously. Surely, oh, surely he wasn't in love with her himself and had kept silent about it all this time? No, you always knew when a man was in love with you. All the same, she wished now she hadn't said it; a few moments ago she had been so carefree. . . . Oh, don't be an ass! Go on thinking about Edward, go on talking of Edward and of marrying Edward—" ' The bride was given away by her father,' the bride's father didn't want to *keep* her, he wanted to give her away, a thing of no value —isn't it an odd way of putting it?" And, from a heart full of gratitude for Edward's very existence, she burst out: "Oh, Geth, it's natural, isn't it, and now you've seen Edward for yourself you'll understand, that after Jackie had ratted on me I should want everything this time so utterly, utterly different. Though he doesn't carry on like the knight-in-armour sort of chivalry, he's more chivalrous to women in the real sense than a lot of tilting and galloping; because when I confessed to him—I had to come clean—he realised at once that going berserk was only the outcome of the awful thing Jackie had done to me——"

" The awful thing Jackie had done to you! And did you also tell him about *the awful thing you did to Jackie?* "

What could she possibly have said to trigger off this

volley from Geth? And not even in his own voice, light and pleasant and amused. Or was it indeed his own voice? But there had been no special nearness between him and Jackie . . . he hadn't been back to England for years and years . . . he had been continents away until a long time after Jackie's death. Stunned and bewildered, Zillah had forgotten something Susanna and then Bridget had remarked, of a much older brother indulging a youngster of twelve, and Jackie's own revelations of Geth giving him a night-light. . . .

And as though she had asked aloud how he could possibly know what she had done or not done to Jackie, he replied with a sombre: " Because I was with him when he died."

" *With him?* "

" He begged his C.O. to send for me. He'd gone out on his own against orders, got mixed up in what's called an incident, shot through the heart or near enough to make no difference. Death wasn't instantaneous, so I'd time to get there from West Africa. After a few days there was a fatal secondary hæmorrhage."

" I don't believe you; they'd have had to let us know how it had really happened——"

" Richard did know; he kept it from Mother and all the rest of you. So you hadn't bedded down with any other man until Jackie ratted on you? I'm afraid, Zillah, your coming clean to this Edward of yours slipped into less than the bare truth, because Jackie's cruel desertion could hardly be held responsible in the case of David; you flung David at him on the evening *before* your wedding day —Oh, your infallible ' face up to it '! He loved you, you were his one love, he was virgin, though nobody would have thought so who'd heard him swaggering just for mischief and a touch of bravado added for good

measure; Jackie was pure gold, single-minded, the only
one of Susanna's four children without a real flaw. Also
you might have noticed, my little darling, if you'd ever
been capable of noticing anything, that it was hardly a
perfect moment to administer any sort of further shocks
from your store of amateur psychology. Jackie was no
coward, but he wasn't by nature equipped to cope with
war in anticipation; he would have recovered his courage
and poise in action, but he should have been gentled over
that crucial moment when he needed a night-light, not a
blacker dark. Scornful of night-lights, weren't you? And
not thinking of Jackie, only of your influence over Jackie,
your juvenile theories of what Zillah believed that
Jackie most needed. But after your ' bracing ' treatment,
your determination to make him ' face up to ' the realism
of war, he had had to prove to himself that he wasn't
afraid, settle it once and for all. So he saw a chance and
went out on his own against orders. No, he wasn't
accusing you even when he lay dying" . . . Geth had
walked over to the window and was standing with his
back to her, staring out as though the partly screened
hospital bed at the end of the general ward were just
beyond the glass. . . ." Naturally he wanted to tell one of
his own people why he'd been such a reckless young
idiot."

Without turning his head to look at her, Geth sensed
nevertheless that Zillah had recovered from her voiceless
impotence to defend or attack, and was about to hurl
forth all her strength into melodrama. He couldn't blame
her; in moments of sheer hate you don't search for
subtlety.

But she laid hold of what she thought more effective
than " I hate you"—" Yet with all your love of Jackie
and all your wonderful understanding that he needed

special protection, you yourself quitted, never saw him for eight years, never came back to England——"

" Never saw him. Never came back to England. Do you suppose I didn't have to force myself to keep thousands of miles between us? I *was* protecting him, the only way I could, by staying away" . . . And let her deal with that, Geth reflected, she who always jabbered so eloquently on the incestuous affiliations in Greek drama, and when she had the theme in her very midst, failed to recognise it.

Going, was she? By now she had got her sandals on, by now she was at the door declaring that never, never again while she lived would she—

—" Cross my threshold? All right, all right, we can take it as read: Jackie ratted and I'm a quitter. Meanwhile you'd better let me get the car out and drive you back to Cobblers Meadow."

" I'd rather walk every step of the way—I'd rather wait hours out in the rain for a lift——"

Geth shrugged his shoulders. He heard her loud defiant song-without-words as she banged away, and couldn't know it was the Zillah-tune. . . . The door crashed behind her; he dialled the bus station to check up on the time of the last bus; looked at his watch—she'd easily catch it with about ten minutes to spare. His hands shaking as they were now, just as well he wasn't let in for driving the car.

——There was the wet scarf she'd thrown off on entering and left lying on the carpet—a pattern of little figures prancing about and saying *bon jour* in every language. . . .

But her limitations were ludicrous: even now she hadn't grasped what she had done to Jackie, any more than why for Jackie's protection he himself had chosen to stay out of reach and out of England all these years. She was mortally afraid, but only because he alone knew she had lied to Edward when she said that Jackie's desertion on their wedding day had been responsible for all her lovers, every one of them, Michael and Tommy and Michael and Brian and John . . . and David.

Revenge was outside his intention. Perhaps when she simmered down she would remember how he had said as much, not in that context but the promise must strike her as significant: " No, Zillah, I won't give you away."

Chapter Thirteen

Yet she was puzzled as to why Geth had not already informed on her: that suspicious invitation for Edward to lunch at his Club when he didn't even know him, and for such an unconvincing reason, and she, Zillah, not permitted to be present. Why hadn't he betrayed her at once?

And then the abominable solution striking across a sleepless night: he had planned to postpone his revelation till the very brink of her wedding day; behind his sinister reply to her light-hearted " I'd have liked you to give me away, Geth "—" No, I won't give you away, Zillah! " lay an intention of timing it in cold blood, a repetition of the former debacle.

But *Geth*? One simply couldn't believe it! Geth, who, though he had teased her, had always been her friend, kind and affectionate? Geth with all this devilry churning inside him? Oh, what a malignant thing to postpone revenge until " a favourable moment," when by telling Edward about David, he could destroy her peace and shatter her future happiness for ever and ever.

And once it had leapt full-grown into her mind, she had no doubt whatsoever. Geth wasn't sane. Geth of all men wasn't quite sane!

Poor little Jackie! You had to be genuinely sorry for what he had had to go through. Highly strung, Geth had said; nervous tension; but she had honestly done her best to help him on that last evening when he had exposed his nightmares. Poor Jackie . . . spare a moment for pity. And Geth should, yes, he *should* have come back if he were so concerned about him and understood him so well; come back to look after him and protect him from the consequences of his over-excitable imagination. The reason he gave for staying away during eight years was—adolescent!

Of no avail to wish and wish you hadn't gone so innocently to Whistle Cottage this evening, because anyhow he meant to enlighten Edward, and then you wouldn't have found out that your marriage was threatened till too late, till after the disaster; whereas now, now you must and would do something to avert it; now you were fiercely determined to fight for your children, fight for Edward, use any life-line that might present itself.

(. . . If Geth could be swatted flat against the wall with the palm of her hand; not murdered, not hurt, just eliminated.)

But she would have to be quick, her happiness was in jeopardy. At the eleventh hour he would act, believing he had a secret mission to avenge Jackie. Rack your brains, rack them hard, think of something. . . . *There was I, waiting at the church.* . . . *I can't get away to marry you to-day.* . . .

Could she *use* that, her mortal dread that the same thing might happen twice? Use it instead of being helplessly tormented by this knowledge of impending catastrophe? Supposing she went to Edward . . . like the plot of a story it filtered into her mind . . . supposing she went to Edward and told him that her previous ghastly experience had left a scar on her, the tissue had grown over it and she hadn't realised until now how all the wedding preparations would start it throbbing again: " Oh, Edward, I'm a coward. I can't face the details: putting on my wedding dress,

with your mother to help me of course, but Susanna too—
like last time—driving to the church alone with Daddy—
like last time—and wondering if I'd have to wait again till
the bridegroom arrived. Edward, it isn't a lack of faith
in you; I trust you with every shred of my heart and
mind and soul; I know *you're* different; but getting ready
for the wedding itself can't be different, even though it's
in London from your parents' house with your sister as
bridesmaid and only about thirty or forty guests, certain
things still have to be the same—presents arriving and
telegrams and bells—Edward, I can't bear it! Please,
please let's get married instead by special licence a few
days earlier, nobody knowing. *Couldn't* we? Heather
would be silent as a clam if I explained, and drive me up
to London in the small hours, and she and I could spend
the rest of the night in some little hotel and meet you at
the church with the special licence in your pocket. Oh,
Edward, *please!* "

. . . Yes, but against that, might be your love for
Edward; if he set himself to coax you out of your goblin
fears, coax you out of your obsession in supposing that like
Jackie he might not turn up at the eleventh hour—" I
couldn't tell him why I'd really be in such a blind funk
of Geth informing against me that my lovers had been
because of what Jackie did to me, *all but one*, all but
David." Men were so strange over all-but-one; even
Edward might become " men " over all-but-one. . . .

Far away the clock at Oldbridge Town Hall struck
three and, a minute later, the grandfather clock in the hall
struck eleven. (Richard had promised Susanna he would
have it seen to!) A bedroom door opened and she heard
Richard go along the passage to the lavatory.

Richard! Her father. Richard's bones wouldn't be likely
to turn to water at the mere sound of Edward's voice. If

she were to go to him rather than to Edward himself and implore him to act as go-between, wouldn't it all sound infinitely more reasonable? " You know how absurd girls are " or " You know what these things mean to girls "— as from one male to another. Yes, go to Richard and pray and pray that he might understand; he did sometimes, and lately he had looked at her once or twice in a worried sort of way, and was obviously relieved at the advent of Edward. She would tackle Richard in his study and confide in him, beg him to intercede on her behalf. And if he thought her desperately foolish, well, he had always thought her desperately foolish, more or less.

Instinct gave its curiously reliable sanction to this plan.

And to Zillah's amazement, her father proved un-expectedly co-operative in what had been at best a desperate measure to enlist him as an ally. He would have preferred a frank readjustment of the present plans, and both families, not only Edward, told the reason for this quiet wedding by special licence a few days before the date already arranged; but it would be hard labour to talk Zillah out of her intrinsic preference for histrionics, so she might as well have it her own way. A bad business, that desertion by young Jackie two years ago!—she told him now that some swine had taunted her, as she passed in the street, with the tag of a music-hall song: *There was I, waiting at the church.* " Why the hell didn't you tell me when it happened? I'd have dealt with him." And Zillah whispered, " I couldn't bear even you to know then! " (Besides, it wasn't true; at least, true in a way, except that it had been flung at Bride, not herself, and it hadn't been the same song but " At Trinity church I met my doom "—Had Bride only told her of having been afraid it might be flung at her, or had it actually occurred?)

"All right, my dear, I'll go up and see Saxton. I don't anticipate any difficulties; he's an understanding fellow. ——Here, stop, you're throttling me!" Richard never cared for embraces, except Susanna's.

"Daddy, oh, thank you, Daddy! Daddy, you so seldom go to London. What will you tell them here that you want to see Edward for?"

"Settlements," replied Richard briefly.

And still more amazing, that he was to prove so resourceful in facilitating all the mechanics of her secret flight to London in the dead of night: send her over to the Brown House for a short stay with Heather, provided with a plausible reason (Fancy *Daddy* telling lies on your behalf!) "I expect she'll miss Zillah more than any of us; Montevideo's a long way off"—Seeing that her luggage for considerably more than a week-end should be secretly stowed away in the boot of Heather's car and for the rest of it to be delivered at Southampton to await them when they joined the boat; and, most important, have a private word with Barry that if he or Don heard the engine at about 1.00 a.m. not to take any notice, not attempt to ask questions nor try to stop them, and to hit Mrs. C. over the head if she tried, which was unlikely for she always slept sound and heavy. And booking rooms for her and Heather at a secluded but expensive London hotel, and arranging for the night porter to admit them at a some-what unconventional hour—all things you might not have thought of for yourself. If Daddy had been always like this——Oh, well, never mind, the vital thing was that he had come to life now when she most needed him.

. . . Sometimes Richard Collier had wondered why the brusque and apparently heartless behaviour by Susanna's son had left no more visible trace of damage on Zillah's psyche; except when after an interval and on the freedom of a legacy to blue, she had run wild in a period of assorted love-affairs, " gone berserk " she chose to call it. He had consulted Susanna but privately did not agree with her interpretation: " young folk talk a lot of hot air." However, anything for a quiet home, and as always, Susanna came first. Lacking a daughter fixation, therefore, in the style of Mr. Barrett of Wimpole Street which might have stirred him to kick young men out of the house, forbid them the portals, and inquire the price of a reliable chastity belt, he had deliberately kept his head averted, and covered his ineptitude with an excuse of not supposing for a moment he had any influence over her—" I'm a rotten bad father! " In her recent derelict phase he had been more disturbed, more quickened to tenderness and inclined to think it his duty to take a hand, than previously when her highly-coloured fantasies had swelled day by day into more outrageous proportions; though the spectacle of a listless forlorn Zillah doing what had to be done but lacking all zest in life was far more the effect he had expected two years ago. Ought he then to have intervened, called her into his study and asked her what was the matter? Yet why had not the rest of his household noticed anything amiss? They had once seemed so fond of the girl.

His first marriage had been a mistake, but did not endure for long; and while Zillah's Grannie was still alive there had seemed no imperative need for him to make different arrangements for the child's welfare; but after her death, and from a sense of duty to this wayward, enthusiastic and thoroughly exhausting daughter of his, he wondered if he should immediately marry again. If he had, there would have been no Susanna, and that

would have left the creeping years too hollow to con-
template; Susanna, fulfilment of all a middle-aged man
could desire, leaving him no room even for an occasional
wish that Zillah, when she was with them, need not
interrupt quite as incessantly nor hold forth as extra-
vagantly. And the Jackie affair was complicated by
Jackie being Susanna's son. He had contrived to appear
characteristically masculine and uncommunicative over
the true facts presently received from Jackie's C.O., and
further private information two years later from Geth
Dymond. In neither case had Zillah's name been
mentioned.

But Edward Saxton, when he turned up, was the
solution to all problems, the right man for her, and South
America the right destination. And Zillah's underlying
motive for a run-away match was neither hare-brained
nor over-romantic in essence, though maybe unnecessarily
Zillah-esque in its accessories; because, although the actual
wedding was not this time to be at Cobblers Meadow, it
was bound to involve a hundred echoes of those preparations for a previous occasion on a bigger scale. Nor
did he particularly want to array himself again in the
ceremonial garments as the bride's father; Susanna had
persuaded him into buying a grey top hat to wear for the
Jackie-Zillah wedding, and he would have had to hoik
that out. Where the hell had he put it?

And God knows what mood Zillah would have produced
when he drove to the church with her to give her away.
In fact, this whole new scheme of hers was a damn' good
notion.

Like a dream that she should actually be on her way to
London at dead of night, on her way to marry Edward
and be with him, his wife, for ever and ever. Like a dream,

except that everything was running without a hitch, and in dreams they never did; dreams turned to nightmares . . . and you suddenly discovered you had no clothes on, or that the driver beside you was not Heather but a Rajah or a cockatoo, and you were in a milk cart and not heading for London but already on the borders of Wales. . . .

Richard had been so swift and competent over the arrangements, that Zillah had not even to write long letters to Edward; and thankfully—what a queer thing to be thankful about!—had received only one letter from him: a few lines to say he thought it an excellent plan to cut out a conventional wedding, and had got it all fixed up with the Rector of a London parish who had known him since he was a boy, to marry them quietly by special licence in his church some distance away from the Saxtons' home; moreover, he wasn't even disclosing to her or anyone else where they were to spend their five days' honeymoon now set free before they sailed from England, but leave it for a surprise.

A honeymoon thrown in as part of this incredible future from which all bleak apprehensions had been lifted away!——Already to-morrow had crossed the border into to-day, and she was no longer on the eve but in and part of it, the most shining to-day of all her life. Her only acknowledgment to the existence of a Geth lying asleep in his bed, was a resolve, as they drew near the poplar beside the pathway that led to Whistle Cottage, not to turn her head in that direction, try not to give as much as a glance which might recall that last cruel hour she had spent there——

" *Stop!* God, it can't be! *Heather*, stop! "

Heather jammed on the brakes and pulled up. Before she had time to ask what danger was advancing from behind to account for this urgent shout from Zillah, she, too, saw an unnatural light leap and fall from a dwelling ablaze less than a quarter of a mile away on their right--and now that the noise of the engine was silent, heard a faint crackling sound. . . .

" *Whistle Cottage!* " And from both at once: " Where's Geth? "

. . . Out of the car by now, but before Heather could follow her impulse to rush in that direction, Zillah's voice again stopped her: " Get back in the car. Drive on. There's a call box on the left before you get into Downsleigh."

Heather was already back in her seat. " It's an A.A. box, isn't it? " fumbling in her bag for the key—had she brought it?

" No, you'll need four coppers? Here——" Zillah handed them to her. " Ring up——"

"—the Fire Station."

" Yes. But Geth first."

" *Before* the Fire Station? "

" He can't hear anything with his deaf ear; if he's asleep lying on his good side, the loudest thing to get through would be the phone ringing beside his bed."

Heather still hadn't tumbled to it. Not impatient with her, but in as few words as possible, Zillah explained: " It's important to wake him first so that he can get himself out. You won't need coppers for the Fire Station; dial Emergency."

" Aren't you coming too? "

" No, one of us should be here in case he——Go *on*, Heather! "

Her hands shaking, Heather turned the ignition switch. " Geth's number! I've forgotten."

" Downsleigh 1685."

Heather repeated, " Downsleigh 1-6-8-5," let the

clutch in, and the car shot away. " It's a matter of life and death." She went on repeating automatically: " A matter of life and death " till she reached the call box. It was there . . . but suppose it hadn't been! Nonsense— nobody walks away with call boxes. Besides, Zillah had said it was.

Wait till she's over the brow of the hill, then pelt along the path. See for yourself what's happening from as near as you can get. He may be hurt and unable to move, or if she'd been right about lying asleep on his one good ear —Dodging the sparks she ran round to the back, stood under his window. Hell, it was *shut*. How queer. Shut, so what chance of waking him by shouts or throwing up gravel? The phone call was the safest bet. But—surely by now and from here she ought to have heard it ring, even through a closed window? What could be the delay? Out of order? Well, then, with Heather not here to stop her and insist on " doing it too," whatever had to be done—no heroic rescue—only a question of waking him—any fool could do that!——

A bell pealed shrilly through the room, cutting the night silence. . . . " That's torn it! " Geth stood debating what he should do, trying to fight down that universal com- pulsion at all costs to answer the phone. Persistently the impact on his nerves went on—till as though the sound had suddenly given him the jolt he needed back to sanity, he strode in from the bathroom where he had just got into his pyjamas, and lifted the receiver. " Hallo. Downsleigh one six. . . . Heather! . . . What? . . . *On fire!* . . . God, yes, I hear it now—how I could have slept through it. . . . Right, you ring the Fire Station and I'll clear out. . . . *Who's* outside? . . . *Zillah!* " He dashed on to the landing.

172

The flames were licking up the hall now . . . an uncanny noise like rending sheets . . . scorching heat and a hideous sour smell . . . crash and thump as the old beams began to collapse. . . . The stairs would go in a moment: if he'd not been lame he could have leapt. A wave of suffocating smoke belched up to meet him from the hall. . . . Back to the bathroom, grab a towel, soak it in the basin already filled with water—*Blast!* He'd tripped over the flex trailing through the doorway—throw the lamp on to the bed as you pass. By a miracle the stairs still held, the front door stood open and he was able to take a long gasping breath . . . before he saw Zillah's body just inside, slumped across the threshold.

Chapter Fourteen

AFTER Richard Collier had identified his daughter's body
in the mortuary, immediately prior to the inquest held in
an upstairs room of the White Hart at Oldbridge, he was
the first witness called to take the oath and give evidence.
The elderly solicitor acting in the capacity of coroner
had known him personally for some time, and treated
him therefore with consideration for his ordeal; so
following the official " You are Richard William Collier
. . ." his tone was not wholly aloof when he inquired:
" Can you tell us, Mr. Collier, why those two girls
were driving up to London alone at such an unusual
hour? "

Richard had expected this and was ready with only as
much detail as might prove necessary. It was he who
had carried the news up to London, and he was anxious
to spare Edward Saxton from the comments bound to
ensue if the proceedings were reported beyond merely the
local press. No, he replied, there was nothing clandestine
about the expedition; he himself had facilitated their
departure just after midnight from the Brown House; his
daughter had had reasons for preferring a quiet wedding
by special licence to the wedding in preparation from the
house of her fiancé's parents next week; and he had
sanctioned it and arranged it with the bridegroom;
perhaps the coroner would accept his word that these

reasons were personal and had no bearing on the actual fire and its tragic consequences? The coroner was satisfied; and Richard, having successfully underplayed the drama of five nights ago, stepped down amid murmurs of sympathy from those few members of the general public who had strayed in and sparsely occupied the back part of the room. For expectation was low, of sensational features likely to emerge; and if there were anything the general public eschewed, it was a straightforward case without sensational features. Those who knew Richard well, for instance the Czelovars, remarked that he was considerably less granite than usual in voice and demeanour; he groped his way along the front row of chairs to where they sat with Susanna, and she held out her hand for him to grab tightly; he had forbidden her to come, but she had overridden him; Richard would need her silent comfort, so all the forbidding in the world would not have kept her away.

The next witness called to the stand was the doctor who had performed the post-mortem, formally to establish the cause of death. This had been instantaneous, caused by a heavy blow on the head when a falling beam struck her as she opened the front door. Then the chief witness was summoned: Mrs. Collier's niece, Heather King, who having been the last to see the dead girl, knew most about what had happened. Heather was crying, so it was difficult for her to be coherent, and the fatherly coroner bade her take her time in relating the sequence of events from the moment they had set out in the car, till, obeying Zillah's instructions, she had driven on alone, found the lighted telephone kiosk beside the road, and after a little delay got through to Whistle Cottage—" though it seemed ages before Geth—before Mr. Dymond answered; one of the pennies was bent and I had to force it in. Oh, and before that, I had had to try and remember his phone number in Zillah's funny way; it wasn't in the book because they'd given him a new one when he moved in, and it had gone right out of my head."

" In Zillah's funny way " required explanation: " She said she'd got it from a famous authoress who told an interviewer that when there were four numbers, and there usually are, like one-one-eight-six, she imagined two people walking side by side, say a little girl and an old man, aged eleven and eighty-six, and she'd say to herself, well, it couldn't be his grandchild if he were that age, his great-grandchild perhaps; and so she built up a sort of collection of little pictures—Zillah, I mean" . . . Heather was being rather long-winded over all this, and the coroner did not pull her up at once; but gently brought her back to repeat her rapid dialogue with Geth, followed by an Emergency call to the Fire Station who told her they had seen the glow in the sky, located it more or less, and a couple of engines were already on their way. No, she hadn't thought Zillah would try to get into the house or she would never have left her, *never*, though Zillah had ordered her—" not a bit in her usual voice, but somehow clear and quick and cross "—to drive off top speed because Geth—because Mr. Dymond—" I'm sorry, but it doesn't seem natural to keep on calling him that "—because she, Zillah, had remembered at once that he had been from birth totally deaf in one ear and that if he were lying asleep on the other ear, the one he could have heard with, only the phone bell ringing next to his bed would wake him——" Anyhow," in answer to a further question, " I didn't think she could have got near enough to his window to shout or throw up things, and I don't know why she tried to get in unless I took longer than she'd worked out." And Heather repeated:

" I'd never have gone and left her if I'd thought——
Perhaps she guessed I wouldn't and that was why——"
She broke down.

" *Mr. Gethyn Dymond.*" And limping up to take
Heather's place as she descended from the stand, Geth
gently put his arm round her shoulders and handed her
over to Barry. The spectators in the back rows whispered
as they noticed with interest that he was wearing slippers;
the interval of time which had elapsed had barely allowed
his feet to heal sufficiently for him to be able to walk; one
of his arms also was swathed in bandages and rested in a
sling.

". . . and nothing but the truth. So help me God."

" You are Gethyn Dymond? "

" Yes."

The coroner expressed a hope that this final witness
might be able to enlighten them on the cause of the fire,
but no valuable information was forthcoming; they had
already heard from his cousin how it was that, lying on
his sound ear, he had woken so late to the danger around
him; and he was able to add little to supplement the fire
brigade's total ignorance as to how the blaze had
originated, though it seemed likely that it must have
started up in the sitting-room as that end of the cottage
was well ablaze before the flames spread to the other
rooms. He acknowledged that he was sometimes pre-
occupied and apt to be careless in making sure his cigarette
was well and truly stubbed out before he flung it away;
and had been known to toss it into the wastepaper basket;
or he might have left it where there was a draught. Yes,
he did live alone. No, there wasn't a coal fire in that room,
merely an electric fire; it was not a cold evening and he
hadn't switched it on. Yes, he had gone upstairs to bed a
little later than usual. Naturally the phone bell ringing

so loudly after 1.00 a.m. was a shock, and maybe, dazed, he hadn't answered it promptly. . . .

From there he described in unemotional clichés his subsequent proceedings up to the moment when he found Zillah's body lying just inside the open door. He hadn't waited then, of course, to make a close examination for possible signs of life—(the doctor had already corroborated that there would have been none)—his first business was to get her out.

" How was she able to enter without rousing you? Isn't it your habit to bolt the door? "

" No, I don't bother; there's nothing specially valuable in the place except the manuscripts I'm working on, and they'd hardly attract a thief."

" But the cottage is in a lonely spot."

Geth smiled, " Not compared with some I've slept in before I came back to England."

" I gather you weren't insured against fire, Mr. Dymond? "

" No."

Asked why not, he shrugged his shoulders and again replied: " I didn't bother."

A murmur from the back of the room, though not as deeply commiserating as for Richard and then Heather; the half-dozen onlookers were inclined to regard it as slightly eccentric not to insure one's property: " Ah, that explains it! "—explained why only one reporter was present and why no expert had been called to testify as to the cause of a fire from which nobody would benefit.

The proceedings were over; mainly enlivened from the angle of the local Press, by Heather's story of how Zillah managed to remember phone numbers; for you can't get much copy out of a simpleton too lethargic to insure his goods and chattels; posting the cheque a day beyond the allowed fortnight's grace would have been the thing; or any suspicion of foul play; but there was none. The coroner summed up as death by misadventure. And added a few words of sincere sympathy with the dead girl's family.

Chapter Fifteen

GETH THREW aside the *Oldbridge Gazette* with its report of the inquest a couple of days before. Something juicier and more mysterious had happened since the Whistle Cottage tragedy, so less space was devoted to it than the family had expected; and in the column still available they had expanded Heather's account of the quaint way Zillah contrived to remember telephone numbers—" she imagined two people walking side by side, say, a little girl and an old man "—as being of news value beyond a fire without arson.

" The truth and nothing but the truth "—only not the whole truth; fatuous to have arranged everything with such elaborate care to spare your mother the pain of knowing her one remaining son had contemplated suicide, and then to defeat it by your allegiance to the bare rules of integrity, swearing fealty when you own to no Liege Lord.

He had been so dead weary of everything; and only managed to keep going while he believed he must somehow justify Jackie's apostasy, putting them wise to Zillah in all her exhibitions, mischievously summoning everyone to come and look at that enormous mote in her eye. . . .

By what means could suicide plausibly be made to look like an accident? Anything but a revolver shot; impossible to dispose of a revolver after it had done its job, and not leave a trace. Start a fire? The cottage wasn't insured, though he had vaguely meant to do it sometime, so he wouldn't be cheating the insurance company. *Fire* and *insurance*—the words had reminded him of a novel by H. G. Wells he read years ago: *The History of Mr. Polly.* Mr. Polly too, was fed up with life, and further depressed by acute indigestion; he planned therefore to set fire to his premises so as to conceal evidence of cutting his throat, and thus be able to leave his wife provided for; but when he had the house in a blaze around him and was ready to carry out his project and make the necessary slit in his jugular vein, it *hurt*—he began and left off with no courage to finish the job. And that might possibly happen to oneself; rather disconcerting to have Whistle Cottage in flames and then not be able to pull off the rest of the programme. However, this was 1958, and surely one could fix up something more scientific and more infallible than Mr. Polly's rather dubious methods? Lucky that one was *not* insured! An addict for truth and cheating the insurance company could hardly have been made to march in step.

But how could a man have foreseen that Zillah and Heather would have been motoring up to London and passing close by on the road at two in the morning? That phone call, too well timed to dismiss as the irony of coincidence. . . . He had had his answer, his life flung back at him with undoubted intent, and a sacrifice exacted in its place——God, have you only this one pattern in stock?

If the inquest had been a trial, you'd have had to plead *guilty* or *not guilty.* Yet still you felt the greater guilt lay in your treatment of Zillah while she was still alive. No, you hadn't come back from Africa for that deliberate purpose; you don't fracture your femur on purpose, and write *finis* to your active life; but being back, deliberately you had worked to intercept her influence, lay a finger on her fun and mute it.

. . . Dead weary. Start a fire, but with no assault directed against anyone but yourself. Susanna would have sorrowed at the news, but the way you pre-arranged it, a clear sorrow; many women down the ages had had to bear the loss of a son, even of two sons.

Was I a quitter? To stay away from Jackie all those years, believing it was the only thing to do for the youngster's safety, believing—I'll never believe anything again.

On the contrary, my dear boy . . .

You waited till well past midnight before you started the fire at the far end of the L-shaped sitting-room downstairs to allow time for it to spread before you did what was necessary upstairs. The bathroom adjoined his bedroom with a communicating door, and the bedside lamp had a flex long enough to reach into the bathroom; then you filled the basin with water and slopped a lot on to the tiled floor in front of you. Next you undressed, put on your pyjamas but not your slippers; the plan was to cut the flex, lay bare enough of the wire, stand in the water and plunge your hands into the basin holding the wires; the result should be fairly swift . . . already you could hear and smell the fire getting a hold. . . . " The balance of his mind was disturbed "—a merciful verdict in suicide cases.

And then the phone bell rang.

Joke over. So you're not allowed to invite even your own death into your own home when and how and where you wanted it.

They say criminals nearly always overlook one trifling thing; in his case, the possibility of the Fire Brigade alerted by the glow in the sky and brought to the spot before the evidence of his suicide would have been destroyed by the flames, as so carefully planned in order to save Susanna from anguish. It was Zillah, not he, who had succeeded in saving Susanna; Zillah who had halted on her way to get married, not caring what he had done to her in the past nor how he might ruin her future, no clamour of self in the ascendant, conscious only of an all-dominating present tense; putting on no act; keeping her head; sending off Heather without even a hint of what she herself was going to do—" not a bit in her usual voice, but somehow clear and quick and cross."

" Oh, God, let me forget myself "—had she ever made this prayer? But then she had never really accepted herself as an assembly of vivid little advertisements, concentrated and held together by being Zillah. Nevertheless, a passionate advocate for the importance of a birthday which had first introduced on the human scene a darling Zillah personally identified, she had at least restrained mention of it for one whole day; heroism on an absurdly small scale, yet perhaps the beginning of dignity pending her complete self-forgetfulness.

. . . Faint strains of music drifting up from the sitting-room below. They had asked him if he wanted a portable wireless in the spare room which was next door to what had been Zillah's bedroom, but he had refused. Faint strains of music, just audible. . . ." She died to music "—no, *with* music. Maybe everyone dies with music, not only in sentimental opera, and we think it must have been chosen to fit our romantic conception of what would be appropriate? . . . Was this a piece of your own wisdom or one of Zillah's flashes? Nice thing if her flashes were wiser than yours! Let's say that neither of us were all that wise. She died with music . . . and you could still hear the Slow Movement of Beethoven's Ninth drifting up from the sitting-room below. . . . But that had been last night. . . . Time fused into a blurred impression of staying again in a house with other people; it felt strange; true, he lived at Cobblers Meadow before Whistle Cottage was ready for him; different then, Zillah had been here, that maddening girl. . . .

As though it had mattered in what vein her ardent life had chosen to squander itself, till at last it could no longer survive the devastation caused by his merciless scrutiny and exposure. . . . " Unless I marry I mean to adopt lots and lots of children! " Adopt—nonsense! Dread that she might *have* to adopt, dread that she might *not* marry. . . . And when at last it came, her lovely certainty, she had believed that he, Geth, was out to destroy it, and longed for him to be somehow *eliminated.* He wouldn't have given her away to Edward, but her urgency for a runaway wedding proved how frantic her nights must have been since the showdown on her last light-hearted visit to Whistle Cottage. Her last visit but one. . . . Helmeted men running across the grass dragging their hoses, as he staggered out of the cottage with Zillah in his arms.

. . . So quiet here at Cobblers Meadow; they had left him alone for a long time; left him alone to think. For once he rather wished one of the family might come in and talk to him, the sort of trivialities that crop up naturally when you're staying again in a house with other people; visits rationed to half an hour at a time, and every-body supernaturally well behaved, gentle and considerate: " How did you sleep, Geth, dear? " " What do you fancy for your lunch? " " Shall we send up Richard for a chat when you've rested? " And bits of cheerful news decanted from less cheerful news to be kept from an invalid—"You don't want to see the *Gazette*, there's never anything in it worth reading "—as though that would have deceived a fly!—and a quick diversion on to good tidings about your manuscript having been saved; to please Susanna you had tried to show gladness and relief, the normal relief of an author in the circumstances, but you hadn't really cared. Besides, you had something else to do first, something else that must take precedence. . . .

. . . Too early to be feeling sleepy. Was he imagining a scent of roses? When you're staying in a house with other people, roses appear in your room, though you don't remember seeing them brought in; it must have been while he was in the bathroom; they were mostly that very dark-red rose, the outer petals almost black, *glowing* black in the dusk of the room. He turned his head and through the windows, saw a frieze of feathery willows, pollarded and then left to shoot up tall against a narrow strip of brilliant ginger-gold below the darkening sky. . . .

"——Geth, dear, were you asleep? Wake up, here's Dr. Caldwell. Oh, Geth, you're a bad lot! " His mother bent and picked up the paper which had slipped off his knees on to the floor. " Our local rag rejoicing in a *crime passionel*—Bridget will be coming up presently, I'll tell her to bring you *The Times*."

Chapter Sixteen

"Dr. Caldwell thinks you're getting on splendidly," said Bridget, coming in carrying a dispatch-case which she set down beside her brother's armchair; "he says he'll make a new man of you."

"Good; I haven't been infatuated with the man I was. But do shed that unnatural brightness everybody puts on when they've had a conference with the doctor downstairs; I wanted to ask you the name of our father's dear old college friend, something-or-other-Brown? Sleeping partner, I believe, in Thorp and Richardson, publishers?"

"Yes, of course, they're the firm who made such a hit with *Bee-line for Wishful Thinking*. Lester-Brown. Your godfather, wasn't he?"

"No, his second wife had been my godmother; we were out of touch for years, and she's dead now. Augustus Lester-Brown, that's right. Directly I can get to London, I'll fix up an interview with him."

"Do you think Thorp and Richardson might pay you more than Bassetts for this," she indicated the dispatch-case, "when it's finished?"

"*This?* Oh, my rescued manuscript." Geth sounded a very casual parent to his offspring restored to him, but his sister attributed it to fatigue still lying over from the inquest, and to cheer him, announced triumphantly: "Dr. Caldwell says you may have it now, provided you don't fall upon it like a feverish beaver but take things gradually, working a little every day. Mother thinks no, but I agree that it would take your mind off——" She stopped. " Aren't those roses lovely? Actually, Wendy chose and picked and arranged them—' out of character,' Zillah would have said." . . . From the frying-pan into the fire—it appeared impossible to prevent a living Zillah, only daughter of Adam and Eve, from obtruding gaily into every subject.

" Does Wendy intend to train as a rose horticulturist instead of an occupational therapist? "

" Yes, it sounds rather incongruous. She's fallen in love with *Virgo* and with that very dark crimson kind, *Sir Charles Mallerin*. If she did take up growing roses professionally, she could do it now on Great-Aunt Hannah's legacy."

" Whose legacy? " Geth was only half listening; he had not been present at the reading of the Will after Zillah's funeral.

" Jackie's to Zillah. Wendy spilt coffee all over the old lady's pearl-grey dress, so she didn't get her half-share then, he got it all." And Bridget went on thinking aloud: " Funny sort of detour, isn't it? If Jackie hadn't died so young . . . and then if Zillah hadn't died so young. . . . Wendy's too shattered to be glad about the money now, but one can't help seeing the advantages; she's always been difficult, though not as difficult as Zillah made out " —(Zillah again! oh, well, it's just too bad)—" when she insisted on dashing down to Sheridan House just before her wedding, because she'd got some dramatic notion into her head that Wendy was really desperate enough to do herself in if she weren't there to prevent it."

" Yes, Mother told me; the other girls were laughing at her over something to do with her scripture classes."

" Youngsters don't kill themselves as easily as all that; they may talk about it, but they don't." Bridget was hectically lighting one cigarette after another and discarding them half-smoked. Oh, God, she hadn't stubbed out that one properly, it might set the house on fire. Had Geth noticed? No, curious, he hadn't. " Geth, wasn't it lucky your study was at the far end of the cottage and not damaged at all; it was supposed to be haunted, wasn't it? You had one good picture on the wall, would you like it hung up here? " He shook his head. " And the room below is intact too, and the garage and your car; though it's bound to cost you quite a lot before you can live there again. *Why* were you such a mutt as not to insure Whistle Cottage and all its contents? "

" Spare the bruised reed and the smoking flax." But his tone was pleasant, so she continued: " It would have covered all this, and now you'll have to draw on capital, I suppose? " speculating on the state of his ways and means in the privileged fashion of a sister. " Hadn't you better stay with Bassetts unless you're sure of a much bigger advance from Thorp and Richardson? "

" Oh, I'm not going to finish my book, not till I've written Zillah's story "—his tone was not free from a certain relish that had been missing for some time, as taking advantage of Bridget speechless at the sensational announcement, he went on exposing his berserkery: " and I shan't be getting any advance on that at all; on the contrary, I'm offering to pay for its publication: it'll work out at an awkward length, about thirty thousand words, and I've no standing as that type of author. Besides, I want it expensively produced, and with the cost of printing what it is—I hadn't so much capital to start with, as I imagine you know? " she wouldn't, though; all his family dubbed him cagey; " and most of it was eaten up by buying the cottage. I could have lived frugally on the very small income that remained and on my earnings, but now I'll have to squander the lot in one fell swoop."

". . . I think you must be insane," remarked Bridget after a long pause. " Not insuring your home, changing your publisher, refusing to go on with the book and forfeiting your advance. You're not the sort of temperament who could live on Mother and Richard."

" I could for a short while, and for the sake of something that matters more." He noticed that she chose to ignore his most provocative announcement. Was she afraid of a show-down? But she needn't have been; he had had enough of show-downs, and no desire to be cruel in portioning out responsibility for all he had done to Zillah in the past. . . . You begin to learn the need for sanity, humility and minding your own business.

But to Bridget his reckless attitude was completely incompatible with the Geth who had arrived in England a few months ago; though, after the brief exhilaration inspired by a boyish desire to get a rise out of his sister by letting her in on his insolvency, melancholy descended on him again . . and she recalled Susanna, or was it Richard, saying that they were apt to forget Geth was still a comparatively young man, seeming older than thirty. She hoped that cloaking her true reactions in an appearance of solicitude, she might be able to deflect him from his purpose, demolish this quixotic madness which had taken possession of him: Zillah did save his life, yes, but then plenty of people saved plenty of people's lives every day —you only had to look at the papers—and one had to be realistic. Impatiently she wondered how long she would have to maintain for the sake of decency this *de mortuis* convention? " What are you going to call the girl in your Zillah story? "

" Zillah."

" *Zillah?* "

" Of course."

" But then everybody will know whom you mean."

" That's the object of the exercise."

" But either you write a work of fiction or a *roman à clef*. What's the idea of a *roman à clef* and the key handed out with the *roman*? "

" Call it a penance."

" A penance! Anybody would think you were a Roman Catholic."

" Anybody wouldn't, you know. But even when you're not a Catholic, there are atonements you can make for a failure in charity." How ridiculous to be so desperately weary, so reluctant to gather oneself together for the long effort of explaining. " Did you see an opera by Poulenc called *The Carmelites*? " She shook her head. " Nor did I, but the theme was taken from a true incident of a Carmelite nun, Blanche de la Force, who was killed by a furious mob during the Revolution. She'd been frightened of everything, frightened all her life, frightened of the smallest thing. When the rest of the Sisters in the Convent were captured and sent to the guillotine, she escaped and stood disguised in the crowd, watching the tumbrils pass; the nuns were singing *Salve Regina*, until one by one every voice was silenced . . . and then suddenly another voice took it up loud and clear, the voice of this little coward Sister Blanche at last free from fear, free from her*self*. . . . And they fell on her and tore her to pieces."

" But Zillah wasn't a coward," Bridget objected; " nobody ever thought she was; so she didn't have to establish that she could be brave in a moment of crisis and danger."

He might have known it, she hadn't a clue. What did it matter? Drop the analogy, start in another place: " I'll have to make special arrangements to circulate my book in Mershire and the areas where the most damage has been done, Ruston Copthall, Oldbridge and Long Swynton; I was responsible for turning her into a pearl of a joke with all of them, pulling down her build-up. . . . I'd no right to expose all those little acts she loved to put on. You remember saying Robert Lee-Curtis would spread it all over the neighbourhood for miles around, when we were laughing about her 'Gail' and 'Robbikins'?"— Bridget would not remember because she'd been drunk at the time; thus he could shoulder all the blame: " I traded on the element in human nature that must always prefer a central object for derision more than for worship; and they'd been gradually finding the Zillah-legend go stale on them."

" Who were ' they '? "

" Oh . . . the whole body of membership."

She missed that point too, and how her zeal in propagating his version of Zillah, allied to her special opportunities, house agent and antique shop and social life, made it imperative now for him to write this book and stop the rot.

" I don't see," said Bridget, after pondering on these revelations, " I don't see, all the same, why you need reduce yourself to beggary just to prevent Robert Lee-Curtis from laughing at Zillah. It was all quite good-natured fun, and, anyway, they wouldn't do it now she's dead. If you feel you must perpetuate her name, what about a memorial window instead? "

" That's an idea! She shall have the window as well; she'd love it."

" And you'll write this story too? "

" Yes."

" But, Geth—*why*? "

" To do her justice," Geth replied slowly. . . . Zillah had once plagued him to write a book about her, and he had refused: " I couldn't do you justice, my dear."

THE END

Date Due

c 7 '09		
OCT 2 1 1959		
NOV 1 1 1959		
JAN 2 9 1960		
Ja 4 60		
FEB 3 1960		
FEB 3 1960		
FEB 1 7 1960		
MAY 1 8 '60		
JUN 1 '60		
JUN 1 '60		
Jn 22 '60		
AUG 5 '60		
𝒢𝐵	PRINTED IN U. S. A.	